STO

A ROOM
WITH DARK
MIRRORS

A ROOM
WITH DARK
MIRRORS

ALSO BY VELDA JOHNSTON

The House on the Left Bank
I Came to the Highlands
The White Pavilion
Masquerade in Venice
The Late Mrs. Fonsell
The Mourning Trees
The Face in the Shadows
The People on the Hill
The Light in the Swamp
The Phantom Cottage
I Came to a Castle
A Howling in the Woods
House Above Hollywood
Along a Dark Path

A ROOM WITH DARK MIRRORS

Velda Johnston

A NOVEL OF SUSPENSE

DODD, MEAD & COMPANY
NEW YORK

Library of Congress Cataloging in Publication Data

Johnston, Velda.
    A room with dark mirrors.

    I. Title.
PZ4.J7238Ro [PS3560.0394]   813'.5'4   75–11938
ISBN 0–396–07150–3

To Marion and Joseph Silvey

A ROOM
WITH DARK
MIRRORS

Chapter 1

O_F course I had no knowledge of the three-day nightmare awaiting me in Paris. I had not known even that a waking nightmare could begin like that—in broad daylight on a familiar street, with hazy sunshine falling on still-blossoming chestnut trees and on a stranger who smiled as he spoke of death.

But I did know one thing, even before the big plane left the ground at Kennedy that evening late last May. I knew that, no matter how smooth the air over the dark Atlantic, the flight was going to be a rough one for me personally. I knew that as soon as I saw that my ex-husband had come aboard.

I was stowing a lady passenger's small pink hatbox away in the compartment above her seat—"Careful, dear. That hat's for my son's wedding"—when I became aware of Eric moving down the aisle, tall figure slightly stooped as he scanned the seat numbers. Apparently he had not seen me as yet. Feeling anger and remembered pain, I turned my face away. When I looked back, I saw the top of his dark blond head showing above an aisle seat in the four-across center section.

The 747's doors were closed now. Time for my life-jacket routine. Smiling but inwardly grim, not looking at Eric as I passed him, I moved down the aisle to the bulkhead upon which the movie screen hung, and stood facing the passengers. While the senior stewardess explained over the intercom what I was doing, I demonstrated how to slip into a life jacket, fasten its straps in back, and pull its inflation rings. Fifteen feet away Mimi Deillman, with whom I usually shared a hotel room during Paris layovers, stood at the head of her own aisle and went through the same familiar motions. I knew that her lips, too, wore a smile designed to convey that crawling, life-jacketed, onto the wing of a plane rocking in the black Atlantic would be really little more than a jolly adventure, something one could dine out on for the next two years.

The passengers in the rows of orange-upholstered seats looked back at me, some attentively, some with the boredom of seasoned travelers, some anxiously. I made an automatic note of the anxious ones in my section. When I have time, I try to comfort nervous passengers with a little extra attention. And tonight I would have time. More than a third of the seats were vacant. As often happened, I felt thankful that no part of my Columbia Airlines salary checks had gone into Columbia stock.

And all the time I was aware of Eric Lang, watching me owlishly through his horn-rimmed glasses.

I stowed the life jacket away in its underseat compartment. Jim Henderson was on the intercom now, speaking in the relaxed, almost lazy voice that pilots cultivate. One might have thought he was about to take us on a hayride down a country road. He spoke of air speed, expected arrival time in Paris, and expected weather conditions there—unseasonably warm and muggy. Then he reminded his charges to keep their seat belts fastened and their cigarettes unlit until the warning signs went off.

Smiling, I moved down the aisle, checking seat belts. When I was beside Eric, he said, "Dottie—"

"Please fasten your seat belt, sir." I was sure that he purposely had left it unfastened. Still smiling, I added softly, from between clenched teeth, "And you might keep your lip buttoned, too."

I moved on, past two almost vacant rows, and then paused beside one of the anxious-looking passengers. Perhaps thirty-five and at least fifteen pounds overweight, she was that rarity in this day of plentiful beauty advice—a truly homely woman. Her hair was coarse and dark and curly, and threaded with gray. Her jaw had an odd, lumpy look. She had framed her one good feature, large gray eyes, in pink-rimmed butterfly glasses ornamented with brilliants. Her liquid makeup, no matter what its color in the bottle, had turned orange on her skin.

Her choice of clothes was equally unfortunate. She had gone in for the thrift-shop look—a dark challis skirt, ankle-length and bulky, printed with small yellow flowers, and a matching jacket with a peplum.

3

On a slim teen-ager, such an outfit might have been fetching. It made her look like the mother of the bride at a gypsy wedding.

She said, "Is my seat belt okay?" To judge by her accent, she had grown up somewhere in the New York area—Brooklyn, perhaps, or New Jersey.

"It's fine. Your first trip to Paris?"

"Oh, yes! I'm on a two-week tour. You know? You get a sightseeing tour of Paris, and two weeks at a hotel. I'm going to be at the Hotel Gamiel. Do you know where that is?"

"Yes, it's on the Left Bank."

"At least I hope I can stay two weeks. It all depends on Mother. You see, she didn't want me to go to a place like Paris. She's awfully religious. She goes to Mass every morning. And her nerves are bad."

She paused, obviously hoping I would seek more information about Mother's nerves. But the jets were roaring now. "I hope you can stay the full two weeks." I moved on, smiled at an apprehensive-looking elderly man and told him to enjoy the flight, and then sat down in the single seat opposite the rear galley and fastened my seat belt.

As the plane taxied through the misty May twilight, I looked at the runway markers slipping past, and thought of Eric. This was the third time since our divorce of nearly a year before that he had turned up on my flight. True, each time he'd had legitimate business in Europe, once a conference of city-planning engineers in Rome, and twice an invitation to lecture at the Sorbonne. But on each occasion he could have taken some other Columbia flight, or even used a different airline.

The 747 roared down the runway, lifted. I looked down at the dimly visible mud flats of Sheepshead Bay. How long, I wondered, would Eric continue to turn up in my life? Every time I seemed on the point of forgetting my brief marriage, I would see him, half a head taller than any of the other passengers, coming down the plane's covered gangway or moving slowly up a crowded aisle.

The seat belt sign went off. Time to put on my apron and add a few dollars to Columbia's depleted coffers by selling drinks. While Sara Ames, who had been flying for the airline less than two weeks, moved ahead of me with the headsets, I pushed the drink cart down the aisle. With disappointment I observed that Eric did not take a headset. Instead of watching the movie through at least part of the night, he would be trying to talk to me.

I said to the lumpy brunette, "Will you have a cocktail?"

"How much are they?"

"A dollar." Seeing her hesitation, I added, "Maybe you would prefer beer."

"Oh, that's a good idea."

I imagined her in Paris, scanning the menus posted in restaurant windows in search of what had become almost nonexistent—an inexpensive meal. Smiling, I let down the tray from the seat back in front of her. "Enjoy it," I said, and placed a can of beer and a plastic glass on her tray.

A few moments later I said to Eric, not smiling, "Will you have a drink?"

"Sure. Two." He tried to let down his tray and after a short struggle, from which I stood aloof, finally succeeded. For perhaps the hundredth time I asked myself how a man could be an engineer, and a good one, and yet be baffled again and again by the simplest devices. Eric went through life tugging at stuck dresser drawers, wrestling with can openers, and hunting for tie clips he had failed to fasten properly.

I asked stonily, "Two what?"

"Come off it. You know what I drink on planes."

I did. On the ground, he was a Scotch-and-water man, but on planes . . . I had an unwelcome memory of a plane in a landing glide over the Bahamas. Turquoise water below, and a green island with red-roofed houses, in one of which we would spend our honeymoon. Eric in the seat beside me, one hand holding mine and the other his Manhattan glass. He had said, "It's funny. I'd never think of ordering this fruit-salad stuff in a restaurant. But once I'm in the air . . ."

Now I thought of repeating, "Two what?" But no. Let him win this round of his childish game. I placed two bottled Manhattans and a glass upon his tray, and then moved on down the aisle.

A few minutes later I had to approach him again, this time with a menu. "Chicken or Swiss steak?"

"Which is the best?"

Gripping a pencil hard, I said in a low voice, "We don't cook them. We just thaw them. Which do you want?"

"Steak, I guess. Dottie, listen."

I moved on.

If Mimi had been working my side of the plane, I would have asked her to serve his dinner. But I was reluctant to confuse the new girl by asking her to vary a procedure she was still learning, and even more reluctant to pique her curiosity. And so it was I who served Eric's plastic tray of steak, French fries, salad, and sponge cake, and I who, twenty minutes later, started to pour coffee into his cup.

With the air of one eager to be helpful, he lifted his cup and saucer toward the carafe. "Don't," I said, but already it was too late. The cup, striking the carafe, tipped over and spilled amber liquid down my apron. Ignoring his apologies, I took the saucer from his hand, set it on the tray, righted the cup, and filled it with coffee. How was it, I wondered, that women could be attracted to him? But they were; they certainly were.

Back in the galley I inspected the damage. Only a little of the coffee had soaked through to my navy blue uniform skirt. With a dampened tissue I daubed at the stain. Mimi, dark curls pinned atop her head, dimples flashing in a smile, turned from the coffee urn to watch me. "I saw him do that. You shouldn't be sore." A wistful note came into her voice. "It's because he's so eager to please you that he goes all puppy-awkward."

Mimi knows only that Eric was unfaithful to me. I never told her the details. Consequently she feels I was a fool to divorce him. I said, "I don't want to talk about it."

For almost an hour I poured coffee, removed dish-laden trays, and placed them in the cabinet that would be removed from the plane when we reached the new Charles de Gaulle Airport at Roissy. Again and again as I moved along the aisle, I was aware that the overweight brunette watched me through her pink butterfly glasses, ready to smile whenever I glanced in her direction. How lonely she must be to feel that grateful to anyone who showed any interest in her. Perhaps she secretly hoped that Paris, that fabled city of lighthearted pleasure and romance, would work some miraculous change in her. But no. No matter what giggling hints she might drop to "the girls" back in her shop or office, the odds were over-whelming that there would be no man beside her as she moved through the Louvre's echoing galleries, or sat at a sidewalk table with a bright, I'm-having-a-wonderful-time expression on her face.

Fleetingly I was ashamed of my own cantankerous mood. Perhaps the old saying was right. Perhaps it was better to have been loved—and betrayed—by even a so-and-so like Eric than not to have been loved at all.

The movie came on. Grateful that for the next two hours Steve McQueen would mesmerize most of the passengers into motionless silence, I moved to the single seat opposite the rear galley, turned on the little overhead light, and sat down. The porthole glass beside me dimly reflected my blond hair, cut short just below the ear lobes, and my even but un-remarkable features. Leaning close to the glass, I

8

shaded my eyes. We flew above an undulating layer of clouds, dimly illuminated by starlight. On the tip of the port wing the red light flashed on and off, steady as a pulse beat. I reached under the seat and brought up a paperback copy of *Finnegans Wake*. Since I had bought it in a Madison Avenue bookshop eight days before, I had progressed to page seventeen. At this rate, I might finish it by Christmas.

"I'm sorry about the coffee."

I looked up. He stood with crossed arms leaning against the overhead storage compartment. "Forget it," I said, and returned my gaze to my book.

"What are you reading?"

Silently, I turned the book so that he could see the cover, and then, trying to register complete absorption, turned a page.

"Good Lord. Last time I saw you, it was Kierkegaard. Dorothy, why do you try to read such stuff? You know you don't enjoy it."

I said nothing.

"You're fine just the way you are, honey. Being born into a freaky family like the Wangers is no reason for you to keep knocking yourself out."

I suppose the word freaky is justified. You have heard of the so-called Kallikaks, whose line some sociologist traced through several generations of mental defectives and criminals? Well, the Wangers are Kallikaks in reverse. No point in speaking of the dead-and-gone Wangers—the Colonial governor, the Signer, the Civil War general, the suffragette leader, and so on. It is this generation of Wangers that I have

9

to cope with. My father, until he and my mother died two years ago in a head-on crash on the Taconic Parkway, was considered *the* authority on American Indian artifacts. His late brother John Wanger, who as a young man moved from upstate New York to the middle-west, represented his adopted state for twenty-two years in the United States Senate, and twice narrowly missed his party's nomination for the Presidency. My half-sister Gale, now in her mid-forties, is one of the few women painters whose canvases sell for five thousand dollars and up. My still older half-brother, Judson Wanger, obtained his Ph.D. in biochemistry, spent a year playing the stock market, and then used his winnings to build a private laboratory on a twenty-acre tract near the Wangers' home town of Marsdale.

As for my sister Natalie, eighteen months my elder, and myself, we are products of my father's second marriage, contracted when he was almost fifty. "My two little addenda," my father used to call us. But only I was an addendum. Natalie was part of the triumphant Wanger story. I grew up reasonably good-looking, and reasonably bright—the dean's list in high school, but no Phi Beta Kappa key in college. Natalie grew up beautiful, and so obviously loaded with theatrical talent that even when she was a teenager, the only question was whether she would achieve stardom first in the movies, or on the stage.

By the time I was sixteen, I knew I had no hope of adding more luster to the family name. And so I decided to become an appreciator of the talents of

10

others. I would visit the splendid cities of the world, and see the great paintings, and read the great books. Hence my job with Columbia Airlines, and hence *Finnegans Wake*. If I had to be a mediocrity, at least I would be a cultivated one.

Eric said, "Why not read something you enjoy?"

I laid the book face down in my lap. "Why not leave me alone?"

"You know the answer to that. I've tried to get over us. I've tried like hell. But nothing works."

Exasperated with myself, I realized it pleased me to hear him say that. "You might try staying off my flights. Who is it who tips you off about my flight assignments?"

Eric lies sometimes. When he does, his eyelids twitch. He said, eyelids twitching, "Nobody tips me off. It's just been coincidence."

During our marriage, he had met many Columbia people, ground personnel as well as my fellow crew members. I could have quizzed him further as to which one he called whenever he planned an overseas flight, but I didn't want him to know that the matter was that important to me.

He said, "Anyway, I won't be flying again for a while. For the next year I'll be living in Paris."

"Why?" My heart sank. I enjoyed my Paris layovers. But from now on, always aware that he might appear at the Rue de Castiglione hotel where I stayed, or that by chance or his design I might meet him on the street . . .

"The Cartmill Foundation has given me a juicy

11

grant for a year's study of traffic problems in European cities, so I resigned my job with the Commission." He meant the New York City Planning Commission. "I've sublet an apartment in Paris. There's a small garden for Wolfgang. Otherwise I'd have had to leave him in New York."

Wolfgang was a two-year-old German Shepherd, kitten-gentle with those he loved, lion-fierce when danger threatened. Often I regretted that I had not demanded custody of Wolfgang. After all, he was joint property, acquired during the second month of our brief marriage to guard our Eighty-seventh Street apartment and to accompany us on evening walks in Central Park. And I could have left him with my half-brother. On the securely fenced twenty acres surrounding Judson's laboratory and living quarters, there was plenty of room for another dog.

I thought of him down there in the plane's hold, and hoped that his crate was roomy enough, and that he was not too lonely or frightened.

"Where is the apartment you've sublet?" At least I could avoid the neighborhood.

"It belongs to a friend of mine, Jake Sommers. It's in Montmartre, right off Rue Pigalle."

"That's absurd. No one lives right off Rue Pigalle. Unless—Your friend isn't a procurer, is he?"

Eric grinned. "Until recently he taught mechanical engineering at the Sorbonne." Suddenly he frowned. "What do you know about Rue Pigalle? You haven't been wandering around up there with a bunch of stewardesses, have you?"

12

"Not that it's any of your business, but I usually don't lack for a male escort in Paris, to go to Montmartre or anywhere else."

"Who, for instance? Jim Henderson?"

I thought of Jim, thirty-eight and divorced, up there on the flight deck, checking his instruments now, or drinking coffee, or pouring tales of his amorous exploits into the ears—perhaps envious, perhaps not—of Co-Pilot Richard Gerber, a family man of forty-five.

"Yes, I go out with Jim sometimes."

"You're not serious about him, are you?"

"Scarcely. Being married to one tomcat was enough."

That reached him. His face whitened. "Dorothy, I'm not a tomcat. It was just that once."

I heard an old bitterness in my voice. "And of course if the girl had been anyone else, it wouldn't have happened even that once, would it?"

He lowered one fist and rubbed his chin against it. "You're giving me Hobson's choice, aren't you? If I agree with that, you'll say it proves how important she was to me. If I say you're wrong, that it could have been some other girl, you'll say it proves I'm a tomcat. Either way, I lose."

"Eric, you lost ten months ago. Maybe we both lost. Anyway, it's over."

After a while he said heavily, "Okay. See you in the morning." He turned and walked away down the aisle.

The movie ended. Soon most of the passengers

13

were asleep, many of them stretched under blankets across the wide row of seats. Ordinarily I too would have slept, but Eric had made that impossible. For a while I tried to follow Joyce's intricate word play— the puns, the portmanteau words, the scholarly allusions. Then I gave up. Less than a mile from the airlines bus terminal in Paris there was a bookstore which carried books in English. Perhaps there I could buy a book I had heard of, *A Skeleton Key to "Finnegans Wake."*

I turned out the light above my seat. Now and then I looked out through the porthole. The clouds had vanished. Far below was the ocean, its black expanse sometimes dotted by a ship's lights. Capella, brilliant and many-colored as a diamond in the moonless sky, swung slowly toward the west, followed by Pollux and then Arcturus. Soon I would see the red light of dawn, not from this height merely a glow in the east, but a fiery line extending along the entire semicircle of horizon visible to me.

Then it would be time to go to the galley and prepare to serve coffee, rolls, and moist, heated towels to the sleepy-eyed passengers.

Chapter 2

AROUND ten the next morning I sat in the airlines terminal bus, parked outside the main waiting room at Roissy. Passengers from mine and other flights straggled aboard, carrying suitcases they had reclaimed from the baggage room. A few yards away stood a small Columbia Tours bus. I watched two uniformed young women shepherding their charges aboard, including three small Japanese men laden with about their own weight in expensive cameras, a tall man in cowboy boots and a white Stetson, and my friend Miss Brooklyn, or perhaps Newark. I knew that according to the prices they had paid, they would be deposited at hotels all over Paris, ranging from small places like the Gamiel, where the wallpaper would be none too clean and the elevator erratic, to glittering establishments such as the Columbia-owned hotel where Mimi and I stayed, at no charge, whenever we were in Paris.

Then I saw Eric. He carried a battered but originally expensive oxhide suitcase in one hand—the same suitcase he had taken with him on our Bermuda honeymoon. The other hand grasped Wolfgang's leash. In the hazy sunlight, the dog's coat gleamed like silver.

A taxi drew up in front of Eric. He managed to get the door open. But when he tried to stow Wolfgang and the suitcase inside, one of his ankles somehow became entangled in the leash. For a second or two he leaned with head and shoulders inside the taxi, while Wolfgang, trying to obey his master's command to get in, clawed with forepaws at the taxi seat. Then the driver got out, helped disentangle man and dog, stowed them away on the rear seat, and drove off.

I felt a familiar wonder. Here was a man who could design plans, successful ones, to regulate the flow of tens of thousands of cars in and out of a city. And yet he had difficulty getting himself and his dog into a taxi.

Mimi came aboard the bus, placed her tan suitcase, twice the size of my blue one, on the overhead rack, and sat down beside me. "Why is it," she asked, "that my suitcase is always the last one off the plane? Why is that?"

"Use a small suitcase. Then you can take it onto the plane with you."

"And not have the right clothes if a chance to go someplace really fabulous turns up? I'd rather wait for my suitcase."

Three more passengers came aboard. Then the driver, who had been leaning against the side of the bus, flipped away his cigarette, climbed the steps, and got behind the wheel. We lumbered off. Soon open fields gave way to factories and to public housing apartments, grimly plain except for the lines of colorful laundry strung between fire escape balconies, so that we might have been driving through Queens, rather than approaching fabled Paris.

Mimi said, "I'm beat. I'm going straight to the hotel. How about you?"

"I'll be along later. I want to do some shopping near the bus terminal." No point in telling her that I would look for *A Key to "Finnegans Wake."* That would have reinforced her belief that I, while in many ways likable, was some kind of a nut.

"Anything new with you and your ex? I saw him talking to you last night."

"No, nothing new."

"You know why he may keep hanging on? Maybe it's your Sun Signs."

"My what?"

"Your Sun Signs, yours and his. I read a book about it. You know how people used to say that two people were fated for each other? Well, the scientific explanation of that is that if your Sun Signs fit, one or the other of you is never going to give up."

"Thanks. You've made my day."

"I just don't understand you, Dorothy. I think he's neat."

She did not mean that she considered Eric tidy. No one could think that. She meant she found him attractive.

When we emerged into the terminal waiting room, almost the first person I saw was Eric. He sat on a bench, with Wolfgang stretched out on the floor at his feet, tongue lolling. Evidently Eric had checked the oxhide suitcase. At least it was not with him.

Mimi turned to me. "Someday he's going to get a case of the smarts and fall for somebody who'll appreciate him. Well, see you." She moved toward the opposite doorway and the taxi stand beyond.

As Eric approached me, the dog began to strain at the leash. "I thought you'd at least want to see Wolfgang."

The shepherd was too well-mannered to jump up and paw me, but he was making puppylike noises deep in his throat. Feeling an absurd impulse toward tears, I crouched, shook the proffered left paw and then the right one, and stroked the rough coat.

When I stood up, Eric said, "I also thought we might have a cup of coffee here. Then I'll drop you off at your hotel."

"I'm not going to the hotel right now. I have some shopping in this neighborhood."

After a moment he said, "Come to think of it, so have I. I forgot to get Wolfgang a new flea collar before we left New York, and there's a pet store fairly near here. We'll walk along with you."

Perhaps because I was tired after my sleepless night, I still felt that desire to cry. "Eric, stop it. Can't you see it's no use? Why give us both a bad time?"

"All right," he said finally. "Go do your shopping."

18

He gave a bleak little smile. "But you don't mind if we use the same sidewalk, do you? Wolfgang still needs that flea collar."

"It's not my sidewalk." To take the edge off the words, I returned his smile. "Well, good-bye, Eric."

Carrying my small blue suitcase, I left the bus terminal. As had been predicted, the hazy air was exceedingly warm for May. An hour from now, the wide sidewalk between the building fronts and the row of chestnut trees, some of them still holding tired-looking blossoms, would be thronged with businessmen going home for the traditional two-hour lunch. But right now only a few pedestrians, most of them women, moved through the unseasonable heat. As I passed two chattering matrons, both in print dresses and too-heavy dark coats, I thought of the legendary chic of the Parisians. Oh, they existed, those exquisitely dressed and meticulously groomed women. You saw them along the Rue St.-Honoré, or emerging from the Ritz or Georges Cinque. But they were no more representative of Paris women than Madison Avenue models are representative of New York women. Those two I had just passed would have blended right into the crowd riding the escalator at Macy's.

I crossed an intersection. Was Eric somewhere behind me? Probably, unless that pet store lay in the other direction from the bus terminal. I did not turn to look back.

Seconds after I crossed the intersection, I became aware of a dark green Ford passing slowly along the

19

street. Why I should have taken even fleeting notice of that one car out of the others moving past, I don't know. Perhaps the attention of the men in the car, concentrated upon me, impinged upon my subconscious awareness, even though I could not have said, at that moment, whether the driver was male or female, or whether there were no passengers or a half-dozen.

The car angled into the curb perhaps thirty feet ahead of me. A tall, well-dressed man of about forty got out of the front seat and stood for a second or two at the sidewalk's edge. Then he moved forward onto the subway grating and stood directly in my path. His smile was courteous.

"You are not to move, mademoiselle," he said in French-accented English, "and you are not to scream. I have a gun in my pocket, and if you force me to, I will use it."

Stricken dumb, I stared up at him. Was he insane?

"You are to get in the back seat, mademoiselle, between those two gentlemen."

Slowly I swiveled my head and looked at the car. I could not see the driver's face. He had turned it away. My dazed impression of the two men in the back seat, who sat staring straight ahead, was that they were both dark-haired and stocky. One man wore a brown suede jacket, the other a dark business suit.

"Remember the gun, mademoiselle." The man on the sidewalk still smiled, but his voice was cold now. "Get into the back seat."

My gaze dropped to his right-hand coat pocket. Something cylindrical poked against the conservative pin-striped cloth. Yes, he must be insane. Or perhaps I was. All that was certain was that no one could have reason to kidnap me in broad daylight off a Paris street.

"I will give you three more seconds, mademoiselle."

That sense of waking nightmare dropped from me. The car was real, the men were real, and whatever fate awaited me if I got into the car was real. With my stomach tightening into a cold knot, I took a step backward.

"Mademoiselle, if I must, I will kill you."

"No!" It was a high, thin sound, but not a scream. My throat was so tight that I could not have screamed, even if I had dared to. I took another step backward. "No!"

Something or someone collided with my shoulder and sent me reeling toward the curb. I saw Eric lunge forward, holding Wolfgang on a tight leash with his left hand. His right fist struck the stranger's jaw and sent him sprawling. Fingers fastened around a spoke of a chestnut tree's protective grill, I was dimly aware of the green Ford starting up and moving away down the street.

The man on the subway grating, with the leashed dog snarling only inches from his throat, seemed temporarily dazed. Only his legs made ineffectual motions, as if some nerve center in his brain was commanding him to get to his feet. But at any moment his hand might dart into his pocket . . .

"Watch out!" My voice was hoarse. "He's got a gun."

A police whistle and the pound of running feet cut through my words. I turned to see a policeman hurrying toward us, his young face stern beneath his visored cap. He blew another shrill blast on the whistle.

Evidently the man on the sidewalk was aware of the approaching figure too, for he raised his head an inch or so and called feebly, in French, "Help! Police!"

The policeman snapped, "Control that dog!" Eric hauled the excited Wolfgang backward a few feet. The man on the subway grating had rolled over now, and hoisted himself to hands and knees. The policeman helped him to rise. "What happened, monsieur?"

"That ruffian attacked me!" They spoke in French. I looked at Eric, whose French is only passable, and saw that he strained to follow the conversation. "First the girl approached me, and then the man came up and struck me without warning."

After a stunned moment I cried, "That is not true! There was a car here. This man tried to—"

"You can explain that later, mademoiselle. There is a police station not fifty yards away."

"Oh, let them go." The stranger was brushing the sleeves of his well-tailored jacket. "No great harm has been done, and I have business to attend to. And after all"—he smiled tolerantly at the young policeman—"one knows what the Americans are like."

"I regret, monsieur." The policeman's tone was firm. "A disturbance has been created. A report must be made to the commissaire of this district."

He was right about the disturbance. Not only a second policeman had approached. A small crowd now ringed us, their faces filled with pleasurable excitement. For a fleeting moment the stranger's gaze, dark and opaque, brushed mine. Then he shrugged. "Very well," he said in a resigned tone, "if one must."

We set off down the street, the stranger walking ahead with the young policeman, Eric and I following with the other one, a man of forty-odd. Wolfgang, quiet now, padded between Eric and me. I was sure that if I looked over my shoulder I would see a small crowd trailing us. Again that sense of waking nightmare descended. Only minutes ago I had been a young woman walking along a familiar street toward a familiar shop. Now I was headed for a police station, followed by curious Parisians.

Eric said, "What happened?" Evidently our guardian did not speak English, for the face he turned to us held no understanding, only that look of official suspicion. "What happened?" Eric repeated.

I told him. In his face I saw a reflection of the stark incredulity I had felt when the tall man ordered me into the car. I said, feeling the first faint brush of a new kind of fear, "Don't you believe me?"

"Of course, honey. But in broad daylight! And *why?*"

"We have arrived," the older policeman said.

Chapter 3

THE four-story building, its entrance set above a short flight of steps, was of honey-colored stone. According to a sign affixed to the wall on one side of the doorway, the building housed not only the police substation, but also the offices of the district's mayor. We stepped across the threshold into a large room whose front windows needed washing. Behind a long wooden railing on the right-hand side two women sat typing at desks. Behind a similar railing on the other side a uniformed man of fifty-odd stood at a filing cabinet. Straight ahead was a door with "Commissaire" painted in black letters across its frosted upper pane.

"Wait here," the younger policeman said. "Tie the dog to the radiator." He disappeared inside the commissaire's office.

A bench stretched along the front wall beside the radiator. Aware that my legs trembled, I sat down. Eric tied the leash around the radiator stem, and then straightened. The policeman stood with his alert, suspicious gaze moving from one to the other of us. The stranger, avoiding my gaze and Eric's, pushed up a white shirt cuff fastened with expensive gold links and, with an annoyed-looking frown, consulted a platinum watch. Although they continued their tasks, I was aware that the typists and the man at the filing cabinet kept glancing at us.

The black-lettered door opened, and the young policeman beckoned. With the other policeman bringing up the rear, we filed into the inner office. The commissaire, a middle-aged man with a plump face bearing a shaving nick along the left side of his jaw, remained seated.

His cold, official gaze moved from Eric's face to mine to the well-dressed stranger's. "I must ask you to identify yourselves. You will speak first, monsieur."

"Certainly. I am Jean-Paul Gastand, dealer in antique furniture." He took an ostrich-leather wallet from inside his jacket. "When this episode occurred, some friends had let me off near the Unicorn Shop, where I planned to look at a seventeenth-century Spanish chest." He laid a card on the desk. "Do you know the Unicorn Shop?"

"Yes. My wife bought a chair there last week." To judge by the pain that flitted across the commissaire's face, the price had not been cheap. He looked at the card. "This is your business address, Monsieur Gastand?"

"Yes, and my residence, too. I have an apartment above my shop."

"You were not raised in Paris, were you, monsieur?"

After eight years of high school and college

French, and almost fifty visits to Paris, my ear, too, was acute enough to detect that the man was not Paris-born.

"No, I lived in Avignon until ten years ago. But as I started to say, Monsieur le Commissaire, I had just left my friend's car when—"

The man behind the desk held up his hand. "Later, please. Now, mademoiselle." His gaze swept my uniform. "You are a stewardess? For Columbia Airlines?"

I removed my stunned gaze from Jean-Paul Gastand. Even I found it almost impossible to believe that only minutes ago this poised, elegant man . . .

"Well, mademoiselle?"

"Yes, I'm with Columbia Airlines."

"Your passport, please."

I set down my suitcase, took my passport from my shoulder bag, and handed it to him. He looked at it, gave it back, and then asked, "Where are you staying in Paris?"

"At the International. I always—"

"I know. Columbia Airlines sets aside a number of rooms for its employees."

As the commissaire turned to Eric, I restored my passport to my shoulder bag and then picked up my suitcase. With its familiar leather handle against my palm, I could almost feel that in another few minutes this nightmarish incident would be closed, and I would be just another weary stewardess, looking forward to well-earned slumber in one of the International's smaller and less opulent rooms.

"Your passport, please."

Eric gave it to him. After a brief scrutiny the commissaire handed it back. "So you are a civil engineer. What brings you to Paris?"

My heart contracted. Eric's grant from the Cartmill Foundation. He might lose it if the Cartmill people learned he had been mixed up in a street brawl.

Evidently Eric, too, had thought of the grant, because to my overwhelming relief he said, "I'm on vacation."

"What is your relationship to this young lady?"

After a moment Eric answered, not looking at me, "We used to be married."

I saw a flicker of interest in the commissaire's eyes. He asked, "Are you staying at the International too?"

I sent Eric a silent message: don't tell about the apartment. The police might phone this Jake Sommers from whom he had sublet it, and Sommers, in all innocence, might mention the Cartmill grant.

Eric said, "I haven't registered at a hotel yet."

"Very well. Now, mademoiselle, will you please give your account of what happened?"

"I was walking along the street." With anxiety I realized that my tone was not one of indignant outrage. Instead I sounded tremulous, unsure of myself. "This car stopped, a dark green Ford with four men in it. This man got out and blocked my way. He told me to get into the car, between the two men in the back seat. He said he had a gun, and he did have, in—"

"A gun!" Gastand's reaction, I realized, was completely convincing. No anger in his face or voice, just blank astonishment.

A surge of rage made my voice even more tremulous. "You do have a gun! It's in your coat pocket." In my mind's eye I could still see the circular shape pushing against the pin-striped broadcloth. The material had sagged slightly in the center of the circle. No pipe stem, no small flashlight, could have made just that impression on the cloth.

The commissaire said in a sharpened tone, "Please raise your hands, monsieur." He nodded to the older policeman. The man stepped forward and ran experienced hands over the well-tailored figure, slapping the chest and the side and hip pockets. Stepping back, he shook his head.

The commissaire said in a much friendlier tone, "You may take your hands down."

I could hear the blood drumming in my ears. What had he done with the gun? He could not have given it to the men in the car. The car had moved away almost as soon as Eric had knocked Gastand down. Surely he would not have dared to drop it on the street or into some receptacle here in the police station.

Then I remembered Gastand on his hands and knees on the sidewalk, apparently struggling to rise. In the few seconds while the young policeman's attention was distracted by the snarling dog, Gastand could have darted a hand into his pocket and dropped the gun down the subway grating.

"Now, monsieur," the commissaire said, "please

give your account of this altercation."

"Certainly. As I have said, I had just left my friends' car when this young woman stopped and smiled at me. For a moment I thought she was about to ask me for street directions. Instead she said, 'A lovely day, isn't it, monsieur?'"

While I listened incredulously, the man behind the desk asked, "And did you answer her?"

"But of course. One does not ignore a pretty girl. I said, 'A lovely day for what?' and she answered, 'For anything you have in mind.' And then"—he leveled a forefinger at Eric—"and then this ruffian rushed forward and knocked me to the sidewalk."

Dumfounded, I just stood there. Despite the cold gaze the commissaire turned upon me, I thought, "He can't believe that of me; no one could." And then I remembered the sniggering books about airline stewardesses, and the X-rated movies, and I knew that he could believe it.

"However," Gastand went on, "I can understand how this young man might have acted upon a jealous impulse. After all, if they were once husband and wife . . . Anyway, I will not press charges. I am willing that we overlook the whole matter."

"Like hell we'll overlook it!" Eric's voice was thick with rage. "You're a liar, and if you don't admit it, I'm going to knock your nose down your throat."

"Silence!" the commissaire snapped.

Eric whirled to face him. "I won't let him get away with it! He can't say a rotten thing like that about—"

"Monsieur Lang! Since Monsieur Gastand has

29

taken this generous attitude, I am willing to permit you and this young woman to leave. But if you make threats—"

"I'll do more than threaten!" Eric was pounding the desk now. "I demand that you arrest this man. If you don't, I'll go to the American consul. I'll—"

The door burst open. I saw a silvery streak arch over the desk toward the commissaire's throat. The terrified man, arm crooked before his face, dodged sidewise in his chair. Chair and man crashed to the floor behind the desk. In the split second before Eric seized the dog's collar, I realized that he must have failed to knot the leash securely to the radiator.

The two policemen were hurrying toward their fallen superior. Eric seized my hand and almost jerked me off my feet as he plunged toward the open doorway. I found myself running with him down the aisle between the railed enclosures, with Wolfgang straining at his leash ahead of us. Fleetingly I was aware that the two typists stared in open-mouthed astonishment.

We were already out the front door when I heard an angry shout from one of the men in the inner office. Hand still gripping mine, Eric hauled me down the steps and along the sidewalk. With my suitcase bumping against my legs, I thought despairingly, "Now he's done it." We rounded a corner and ran perhaps twenty more yards. Then Eric drew me inside an open doorway.

Dimness. Chatter of caged birds. Rows of fish tanks, doghouses, and stands displaying leashes and

30

dog collars along each wall. Halfway down the aisles, we stopped, breathing hard. For a moment I thought the shop was unattended. Then from beyond a door at the rear I heard shrill puppy barks, a loud caterwauling, and a man's soothing voice. "Come on," Eric said.

He opened the door. With Wolfgang padding ahead of us, we went into the rear room. Reaching behind him, Eric pulled the door closed. Here light poured through a skylight onto cages holding poodle and boxer puppies, a small monkey, and two Siamese cats. One of the cats, to judge by her harsh and continuous caterwauling, was in heat.

His hand on the latch of the boxers' cage, a small man with graying dark hair and gold-rimmed glasses turned a startled face toward us. Eric and I, I realized, were both still breathing hard.

"Damned dog started chasing a cat," Eric explained. "I thought he was going to pull my arm out of the socket."

As if to contradict that libel upon his manners, Wolfgang sat down. Paying no attention to the noisy Siamese, he gazed at the shopkeeper with polite interest.

"I may serve you, monsieur?"

"Yes, I would like a flea collar. Also, could you board my dog for a few days?"

After a startled moment, I realized why Eric wanted to rid himself temporarily of the shepherd. The dog, like my uniform, made us easily identifiable. And thanks to Wolfgang's loyal though mis-

31

directed protectiveness and Eric's impulsive bad judgment, the police would be looking for us.

Then I realized that perhaps Eric had been wise in hauling me out of the police station. True, Gastand had been understandably willing to have us leave, and so had the commissaire. But the shepherd's flying leap had changed all that. If we had stayed there, we would be on our way to jail now, I for disorderly conduct, and Eric for assault upon a police official with a deadly weapon—namely, Wolfgang.

With my palms turning cold and damp, I heard, muted by distance and the closed door, the shrilling of a police whistle out on the sidewalk. I strained my ears for the sound of footsteps in the outer room. The thought of arrest made me almost literally sick at my stomach. I thought of a magazine article I had read. Its author, a college girl who had been arrested during a political demonstration, had described vividly her overnight ordeal—the fingerprinting, the humiliating physical examination by a cynical doctor, the burly police matron who had bruised her arm leading her to a cell. The procedure in French jails might be even harsher.

And worse than the arrest would be the publicity. Certainly there would be publicity, not because I was an American airline stewardess, but because I was Natalie Wanger's sister and the late Senator John Wanger's niece.

I had never hoped to add more luster to the Wanger name, but I had never expected to disgrace it, either.

The little man was saying, "This is a shop, monsieur, not a boarding kennel."

"Still, couldn't you keep him for a day or so? I would be willing to pay fifty francs a day."

From the way the man's face lit up, I gathered that for fifty francs he would be willing to have Wolfgang share his own bed. "You will pay the first day in advance?"

For answer, Eric took out his wallet and handed the shopkeeper a fifty-franc note. He pocketed it and then said, "Perhaps you noticed the doghouses in the outer room. Your dog may have the largest of them. And regard this, monsieur." Opening a second door, he led us into a small, brick-paved courtyard. A dispirited-looking sycamore tree stood in an angle of the high board fence.

"Your dog can take his exercise here. And I will change his flea collar, of course. For now, perhaps it would be best if you tied him to the tree."

For several minutes Eric and the shopkeeper discussed Wolfgang's diet. I knew that Eric's motive in lingering was more than concern for his dog. Like me, he hoped that by the time we emerged from the shelter of this shop, we would find the street free of police. At last he scratched Wolfgang behind the ears and told him to be a good dog. At these indications that, once more, he was to be left with strangers, the shepherd looked unhappy but calm, as if harboring no doubt that Eric would return for him.

Beside the cage of the noisy Siamese, we said good-bye to the proprietor and moved into the outer room. Hand on my arm, Eric stopped me before we had gone more than a third of the way to the front door. Staring with an air of rapt interest at a tank of tropical fish, he asked softly, "Did you get the license number of that Ford?"

"No."

"Neither did I. What did the men in it look like?"

"I didn't see the driver's face. And I doubt that I'd recognize the other two. I only know that one of them was in a dark suit, and the other one had a brown suede jacket." I paused. "Eric, what are we going to do?"

"Go out on the sidewalk. Hope we don't see any cops. Walk to the cab rank across the next intersection and hope there's a cab waiting."

"But where are we going?"

"I don't know. Out of this neighborhood. Maybe to some café near the Tuileries. Anyway, someplace where we can talk this over."

Nerves taut, I moved with him to the door. It must have been past noon, because now the broad sidewalk was thronged with people, some moving toward the subway entrance on the corner, others in the opposite direction. We looked both ways and across the street. No sign of police. Evidently they had decided that we had gone down some other street.

"Come on. Walk fast, but not too fast."

We turned to our right, moving at a slightly more rapid pace than the crowd of businessmen and chattering shopgirls and office workers. Then, from the corner of my eye, I saw a dark green Ford on the far side of the street, moving slowly in the opposite direction. Heartbeats surging with panic, I averted my face. "Eric . . ."

Evidently he, too, had seen the car. Hand grasping my arm, he hurried me, not toward the intersection, but down the Metro's steps. He thrust money at the ticket seller. Each of us clutching a ticket, we joined the queue at the turnstile. I fought so hard against the impulse to turn my head and look back that my neck ached. Probably there were scores of dark green Fords in Paris, I reminded myself, perhaps hundreds. And even if it had been the same car, perhaps its occupants had not spotted us in the sidewalk crowd.

We pushed our tickets into the slot, moved through the turnstile. We went down more steps. At their foot a small crowd waited behind the gate barring the train platform. Again I had that overwhelming urge to look back and see if a dark-haired man in a suede jacket had joined the growing crowd behind us.

A train slid into the station with that quiet smoothness so novel to those used to New York subways. The platform crowd surged aboard. As soon as the train pulled out, the gate at the foot of the steps opened, and Eric and I moved with the others onto the platform.

The temptation had grown too great. I looked to my right and my left, and then behind me. Weak with relief, I saw plenty of dark business suits, but no one in a suede jacket. A train sighed to a stop. Eric and I got aboard.

The car was crowded. The only seat available seemed to be one half of a bench which, according to the plaque above it on the car wall, was reserved for the disabled and for pregnant women. The other half of the seat was occupied by a blond woman, obviously pregnant, who held a Le Printemps shopping bag balanced on her knees. Eric and I stood a foot or so away from her, facing the door, and grasping a white-painted metal stanchion.

The train slid into a station, discharging perhaps half a dozen passengers from our car, and taking aboard several times that many. When the train again was in motion, I said softly to Eric, "They didn't follow us. If it was them, I mean."

He nodded.

"When shall we get off?"

"Might as well stay on for five or six stops."

We arrived at another station, discharged and took on passengers, pulled away from the platform. Suddenly Eric's hand was on my shoulder, pressing downward. "Sit down!"

Heart hammering, I sat down beside the blond woman and hoisted my suitcase onto my knees. Eric moved in front of me, so that his back shielded me from the view of those who had entered at the car at its far end. He leaned down. "When I tell you to," he said softly, "move!"

I sat rigid, knowing that he had seen someone—a policeman?—a man in a brown suede jacket?—enter the car to join the standees. From the corner of my eye I saw that the woman with the shopping bag kept her face turned toward me. Under other circumstances, the outraged accusation with which she stared at my flat stomach would have seemed funny.

The train stopped. The door near us sighed open. I tightened my grip on my suitcase handle. A woman and a little girl came in. Eric waited perhaps another second. Then, "Now!" he said, and seized my hand. We plunged onto the platform past the edge of the closing door.

Chapter 4

ERIC hurried me, not toward the stairs that led to the street, but down a narrow tunnel. We had gotten off, I realized, at what the French call a *correspondance*, a transfer point between two subway lines. Always I had disliked those transfer tunnels. It was not just that they were lower and narrower and more tortuous than others. The fluorescent lights set in their tiled walls seemed to give off an especially ghastly glow, so that those who moved along these winding underground passageways had the pallor of people newly released from a hospital or a dungeon. Now, when anxiety was like a band across my chest, I found the tunnel doubly oppressive.

I asked, "Who—"

"A couple of guys got on. They were both dark-haired, and one was wearing a brown suede jacket."

I imagined the dark green car driving swiftly to a station two stops beyond the one where Eric and I had plunged down the steps. I pictured them hurrying down Metro steps, then watching the incoming train slide past until they spotted a lanky blond man and a girl in a navy blue uniform, clinging to a stanchion.

We turned a curve in the tunnel. A moment later I heard following footsteps. Even though reason told me that no one could have left that subway car after we did, I had a panicky sense that those footsteps, echoing hollowly between the curving tiled walls, were those of a pursuer.

We emerged onto a platform. Eric and I moved to an already crowded bench and sat down. A few seconds later, feeling foolish, I saw a bearded youth with a back pack emerge from the *correspondance* tunnel. He sat down on the platform, crossed his extended legs, and, despite the dimness of the light, opened a paperbound book and began to read.

A train came in. Again we had to stand. After several stops Eric said, "We might as well get off at the next station. We can't stay down here forever." I looked up at him and saw that his face was as white and strained—and bewildered—as I knew mine must be.

We left the train, climbed steps. I'd had only the vaguest notion where our flight underground was taking us, but now, as we emerged into what was for me familiar territory, I saw that we must have traveled in a semicircle from the Left Bank to the Right and then back again. On one corner rose the medieval tower of St. Germain-des-Pres. Opposite it, sidewalk tables clustered on two sides of the Deux Magots, that erstwhile haunt of Sartre and other French intellectuals. On still another corner stood Le Drugstore, that glittering emporium which, in imitation of California drugstores, offers its customers almost everything from ski equipment to books, and from Scottish sweaters to American-style hamburgers, served in an upstairs dining room elegant with mirrors and gold leaf.

We moved up Boulevard St.-Germain. Here the sidewalk crowd, drawn from the nearby schools of fine arts, architecture, and medicine, was mostly young. Just before we reached the corner, Eric grasped my elbow and said, "In here."

No one at all sat at the café's outdoor tables, baking in the unseasonable heat. In the dim inner room a few young men and girls sat in pairs or alone in the booths and at the small tables, books and papers spread out beside their tiny coffee cups. There was no juke box music, no laughter or even loud voices. Here in France, where only the able and serious-minded can hope to pass the universities' formidable entrance examinations, let alone receive a degree, this student gathering place was almost as quiet as a library. Eric and I moved to a booth at the rear of the room.

His heat-pale face, as he sat across from me at the bare-topped wooden table, still held that bewildered anxiety. When the waitress had brought our coffee and then left us, he said, "I'm sorry. If I hadn't lost my temper there in the police station, and if Wolfgang hadn't gotten loose—"

"I know. But there is no point in talking about it."

40

Besides, no matter how ineptly he had behaved after he sent Jean-Paul Gastand sprawling, I was fervently glad he had knocked the man down. I wondered, with my stomach knotting up, where I now might be —and in what condition—if Eric had not been following me along the sidewalk.

I asked, "What are we going to do?"

His voice was heavy. "Only one thing to do. Go to the police and try to straighten this mess out. But we'd better have someone running interference for us. Otherwise we may find ourselves behind bars for an indefinite period. And French jails, I hear, are pretty rough.

"Much as I hate to suggest it," he went on, "I think you'd better get in touch with Jim Henderson."

Of course, I thought, with flooding relief. The thing to do was to have Jim approach the police. He was not only a valued Columbia employee. His sister's husband was on the company's board of directors. If Jim would mobilize behind us the power of Columbia Airlines, which brought millions of tourist dollars into France each year, the police would look at us through different eyes. Not only would they be willing to settle for an apology from Eric and me, but they might even bestir themselves to investigate Gastand and his antique business and his friends.

"I'll call the International."

I went back to the phone booth, pushed a button, deposited a token. I talked first to the switchboard operator and then the concierge, who told me that Monsieur Henderson had checked in two hours ago, but had left the hotel half an hour later. Did I care to leave my name and a message?

"No, thank you." Doubtless that justifiably outraged commissaire had telephoned the hotel about me. Or, more likely, there was a policeman waiting right now in the gold-leaf-and-red-velvet splendor of the International's lobby.

Despite the big room's comparative coolness, I felt sweat spring out on my upper lip and my forehead as I walked back through the quiet dimness to our table. I sat down. "Jim's out someplace. We'll just have to keep trying."

Eric nodded. "Tell me again what happened after that guy got out of the Ford."

I told him. For a few seconds the hazel eyes behind the horn-rimmed glasses remained fixed on my face. Then he looked down at his coffee cup and began to turn it in its saucer. "What's the matter?" I asked in a taut voice. "Don't you believe me?"

"Dottie, it's just that—"

"Are you starting to believe *him?*" I knew that I was being absurd and unfair, but with my nerves stretched tight, I could not stop. "Do you think that I was propositioning him when you rushed up and—"

"Dottie! No! I know he was lying, and that you were not."

"Then why do you look that way?" I asked bitterly. "What do you think is the truth of the matter? That I was hallucinating?"

"Dottie, listen! Don't you think you might have

42

misunderstood what he said to you? After all, if he has a southern France accent—"

"I didn't misunderstand." My voice was cold.

"But, honey, it just doesn't make sense. Even if they were some bunch of sexual weirdos, they'd go for something less risky than snatching a girl off a busy street in broad daylight. And why else would anyone want to kidnap you?"

Yes, why else? Certainly not for ransom. The Wanger family was distinguished by talent and achievement, not wealth. My father and mother's modest estate, when divided among their four children, had brought us only a few thousand apiece. Almost all of the money my half-brother Judson had made in the stock market had gone into that private laboratory of his. My half-sister Gale, although more successful than most women painters, was far from rich. It was true that my sister Natalie, when she worked, sometimes earned a four-figure salary each week. But more than a year before she and a Hollywood acting couple had been rash enough to pool their money—and borrow heavily from a bank—to produce a little turkey called *Tangled Roots.* Since then, most of Natalie's earnings had gone to pay off the bank loan. No, I would not bring ransom large enough to make the dangerous act of kidnaping seem a worthwhile risk for even one man, let alone four.

I said, "Maybe they mistook me for someone else."

"Maybe."

I could tell he did not believe so. Nor did I, after a moment's reflection. For what rich girl could they have mistaken me, in my navy blue uniform? If there was a Rockefeller or a Getty flying for Columbia Airlines, I had never heard of her.

The silence between us lengthened. Looking down at my almost untouched coffee, I forced myself to consider the possibility that, in Eric's phrase, I had "misunderstood." He had not meant misunderstood. He had meant imagined. Could I have imagined Gastand's words and that gun muzzle poking against the pin-striped cloth? Surely not. I could still feel the profound shock of that encounter there on the sunny sidewalk. That proved nothing, though. The impression left by an—an aberrated interval might remain as vivid in my memory as that of a real event.

But I had no history of mental or emotional instability, nor did any member of my family.

Except of course—I felt a cold queasiness—except for Judson. Sometimes with amusement, sometimes with exasperation, we Wangers called my half-brother eccentric. Some outsiders might use a stronger term.

I thought of his laboratory, with its adjoining living quarters for himself and his assistant, set in twenty acres of pine woods a few miles from Marsdale. Constantly afraid that someone would ferret out the results of his researches before he was ready to publish them, Judson had made the place into a veritable fortress. The chain-link fence surrounding his property was ten feet tall, and topped by a wire guaranteed to give any fence-climber a severe although less than fatal shock. Any attempt to sever the heavy chain links with wire cutters would set off burglar alarms in the laboratory. Not content with such measures, Judson also kept Dobermans. At night, except on the rare occasions when Judson admitted some visitor to his stronghold, the Dobermans roamed through the pines, sleek and deadly as panthers. And no one was admitted through the gates at any time unless Judson or his assistant—younger than Judson, but in his own way just as odd—had made sure of the visitor's identity.

If Judson had worked on projects that might have brought him vast sums of money—a new kind of synthetic rubber, for instance—these precautions against theft of his work might have made sense. But of the three products for which he had sought patents—a cheap vitamin supplement for pet food, a more rapidly dissolving aspirin, and a painkilling drug to be substituted for Novocain—he had been able to offer only the aspirin to prospective manufacturers. The vitamin supplement had been judged too similar to an existing product, and the painkiller had been banned by the Food and Drug Administration as too dangerous. As for the aspirin, it had failed to interest any manufacturer.

Perhaps it was because Judson and I were so fond of each other that I had not, until now, given much thought to his strangeness. In fact, I was the only one of our family for whom he seemed to feel affection. He and my half-sister Gale had never gotten along, even as children. As for Natalie, about two years before, growing overconfident with a fan-magazine interviewer, she had given him some anecdotes about Judson. I am sure that the result, a published paragraph that made her half-brother and mine sound like a candidate for commitment, was not what she had intended. Nevertheless, he had never forgiven her for it.

But perhaps he *was* a candidate for commitment. With my sense of cold unease growing stronger, I remembered a visit I had paid him the previous February. We had sat in the office adjoining his laboratory, he in the swivel chair beside his desk, I in a leather armchair with the stuffing bursting through the seams. Perhaps his laboratory expenses were so heavy that he felt unable to replace the ancient armchair. More likely, it had never occurred to him to do so. Weak winter sunlight slanted through the window onto his graying, ginger-colored hair, his thin, lined face, his blue eyes that always appeared a little tired from squinting through microscopes and poring over notebooks filled with his cramped, almost illegible handwriting.

Even though the door to the laboratory had been open that day, I heard none of the animal sounds I had heard on previous visits—chatter of caged monkeys, rustle of rabbits through straw covering the floors of their hutches. I asked, "What did you do with your animals?"

"Sold them. I don't need them now. The research I was doing is almost finished."

Even though I knew that Judson's experimental animals had never endured those agonies which fill

46

so many people with pity and rage, I still was glad they were gone. I had never liked the sight of those caged creatures. I asked, "What sort of research is it?"

"Allergies."

"You may have a new cure for allergies?"

Thinking of how the face of this lonely man always lit up at sight of me, remembering how when I was a little girl he had read to me, answered my endless questions, and allowed me to follow him about, so that he seemed far more of a parent to me than my already-aging father—remembering all that, I hoped that his allergy cure might meet a better fate than other products of this laboratory.

"What I'm trying to do," he said, "is to broaden the range of allergens."

"Allergens?"

"Substances which when taken into the human system cause allergic reactions—asthma attacks, nausea, edema, and so on. As you probably know, there are hundreds of allergens, ranging from pollen to egg white, and from cat fur to dust."

He went on to explain that some people are born sensitized to certain allergens, and others suddenly become so later in life. "Why this is so," he said, "we are not sure. But we have found that we can artificially induce allergic reactions to cat fur and so on."

I said, bewildered, "And you've been looking for a way to make people allergic to still more things?" It seemed to me that the world needed more allergens the way it needed more cockroaches.

"That's right."

"But why? What good would it do?"

After a moment he said testily, "That's a typical layman's question. The aim of pure science is not to do good. It has no aim. Like art, it is its own justification."

"But, Judson! You're an applied scientist. All those products you've—"

"A scientist is a scientist. It's the direction in which he turns his energies which determines whether he is a pure or an applied scientist. Now tell me, how was your last trip?" My brother seldom ventured even as far as Marsdale, six miles away, let alone another continent, but he seemed to enjoy hearing of my travels.

I left soon after that. Outside I saw Bert Haliday, Judson's assistant, a shy, sloping-chinned man of about thirty. He stood inside the chain-link fence of the Dobermans' kennel spooning dog food from cans into metal bowls. The well-trained beasts watched him hungrily but patiently, neither barking nor trying to snatch their dinner from the table. I said, "Hello, Bert."

Adam's apple working, he gave me a nod and a shy smile, and then went on spooning food out of the cans. I felt a rush of sympathy for him. True, Judson paid him an excellent salary. But in return he demanded that Haliday live almost as reclusively as he did. Twice a week, in Judson's truck, Bert drove up the drive—its surface so chuckholed and rock-strewn that only the truck's high undercarriage could traverse it unscathed—and through the gate to go to Marsdale for supplies. Otherwise he left the laboratory only for his three days off each month. Apparently he usually spent those three days in New York. Apparently, too, he sometimes became thoroughly and understandably drunk while there. One bitter January afternoon Natalie had caught a glimpse of him reeling down Second Avenue, bareheaded, and with his unbuttoned overcoat streaming back in the icy wind.

Feeling annoyed with Judson, I had walked up on the drive. Then, a few seconds later, I had caught a glimpse of a little white building through the trees off to the right, and my mood softened. It was a shed which, during the laboratory's construction, had sheltered building materials. Later Judson had ordered that it be made into a playhouse for Natalie and me. He'd had it painted white, and even installed four-paned windows, ornamented by little window boxes in which Natalie and I planted petunias. I recalled how on many afternoons he had taken time out from his work to join my sister and me in the playhouse, sitting cross-legged on the floor beside a little table while Natalie and I served him "tea," which was actually milk, and oatmeal cookies.

Smiling, I had gone the rest of the way up the rock-strewn drive and through the gate to my VW, parked out on the road.

Until this afternoon, I had thought no more about my last visit to Judson, or his account of his research. But now I found the memory deeply disturbing.

True, Judson's current endeavor probably would prove as ineffectual as past ones. But still, what sort of man spent his time working on something which, even if it turned out to be successful, could only add to the world's miseries?

Perhaps there was something very wrong with my brother. And in that case perhaps I, too—

I said, "I'd better try to call Jim again." I got up and walked to the phone booth.

No, I was told, Monsieur Henderson had not returned.

I hung up and leaned against the booth's wall, eyes closed. As sometimes happens, accumulated weariness suddenly overwhelmed me. I'd had no sleep the night before, and the last few hours had been exhausting in the extreme. Longingly I thought of that room with its twin beds at the International. But no, I could not go there, not until after I had talked with Jim Henderson.

Still, I had to rest somewhere. There was a small, inexpensive hotel nearby on the Rue des Saints-Pères. The summer I was fifteen, my mother and Natalie and I had stayed there for a week. What was the name of it? Oh, yes. The Briault.

With eyes so weary that the fine print seemed to blur, I looked up the number in the phone book. I dialed. Yes, a woman's voice told me, the Briault had a vacancy.

I walked back to the table and sat down. "Jim is still out. Eric, I've got to sleep for a few hours, or I'll fall flat on my face. I've reserved a room at a hotel near here, the Briault."

"I hate for you to be alone. Won't you come to the flat?"

I shook my head.

"I didn't think you would," he said heavily. "And maybe it's just as well. If the cops really try, they'll get a line on me soon enough. I had to take out a *carte de travail* in order to take up the grant, you know."

Of course. He'd had to apply for a work permit. And in France it was the police who issued such permits. Although they probably had not discovered the fact as yet, they had all sorts of information about him in their files, including the address of that flat he'd sublet.

Eric in jail, and no longer with a prospect of a year's study in Europe. Perhaps it was partly because I was so tired that I felt an impulse to move to his side of the booth, put my head on his shoulder, and cry. Instead I said, "I'm sorry you're in trouble because of me."

"I'm not sorry. I'm just glad I was there."

Since Eric had proved himself to be a so-and-so in a very basic way, why couldn't he be a so-and-so in every way? Why did he have to be so darned sweet sometimes?

"Eric, about that Gastand. Do you think I could have—gone crazy for a few minutes?"

He said quickly, perhaps a little too quickly, "Of course not."

"Well, I don't know." I forced a smile. "Maybe Dottie ought to be spelled with a 'y.' I mean, my brother's pretty weird."

"He's only a half-brother." His smile, too, appeared

forced. "So if you're weird, it's probably only a little, around the edges. Come on, I'll take you to that hotel."

I shook my head. Perhaps notification about us had gone out to all the precincts. In that case, the less we appeared together on the streets, the better. "I'll be less conspicuous alone. Just give me your telephone number at the flat. I'll keep trying to get in touch with Jim. As soon as I do, I'll let you know."

"All right. But first of all, get some sleep."

go far. On the next street was a small restaurant which served reasonably good food.

Parisians dine late. The café was less than half full. When I had sat down at a table against one wall of the narrow room, I ordered a glass of Compari and, since I knew it could be served as soon as I had finished my drink, a *ragoût de veau*. I sipped the Compari, trying to enjoy it, trying not to think of Gastand, or the police, or of what might happen to Eric or to me if I remained unable to enlist Jim Henderson's help and protection.

My dinner arrived. I had taken only a few mouthfuls when I heard someone tapping on the restaurant window a few feet to my left. I turned my head. Out on the sidewalk, waving, stood the overweight brunette I last had seen boarding a tour bus at Roissy. I felt dismay at sight of her, but little surprise. The hotel at which she had told me she would stay was less than a quarter of a mile away, on the other side of Boulevard St.-Germain.

I returned her wave. Immediately she moved to the restaurant doorway and came in, wearing that same long-skirted costume. She had added a touch, though, a gold-plated souvenir bracelet from which dangled a miniature Eiffel Tower. Obviously she meant to join me, and although I felt far too weary and sore beset to welcome a dinner companion, especially a loquacious one, there was nothing I could do about it.

"Say!" she exclaimed. "I never expected to see you again! This is wonderful. Is the food good here? The

Chapter 5

RUE des Saints-Pères is one of those twelve-feet-wide Left Bank streets that date back almost to the Middle Ages. As I moved past its antique shops and bookstores, along a sidewalk made even narrower by cars parked with their left-hand wheels up on the curb, I suddenly realized that the police, unable to find me at the International, might have sent my name and description to all Paris hotels. Pulses rapid, I entered the Briault's small lobby.

I need not have worried. The desk clerk, a middle-aged brunette woman, smiled pleasantly, looked at my passport, and handed me a registration card. The porter, a blond young woman so strapping that probably she could have carried a small trunk on her back, lifted my suitcase as if it had been an empty shopping bag. She rode with me in the tiny, creaking elevator to the second floor, where she deposited the suitcase in my room, handed me a key, and thrust my tip into the pocket of her blue porter's smock.

An afterthought struck me. Eric might phone

before I'd had the several hours' sleep I needed. "There may be a call for me. Will you please ask the lady at the desk not to put it through? I want to sleep for a while."

"Certainly, mademoiselle."

When she had closed the door, I looked around me. The room was much like the one my sister and I had shared eight years before—small, with faded floral wallpaper and an even more faded floral rug, and only one window, opening onto an inner courtyard, so that the light was dim. But the bed looked comfortable, and anyway, I could have curled up and gone to sleep on the floor. I looked into the disproportionately large bathroom with its huge old tub, but decided against a shower. That could come later. I took off my uniform and hung it in the old-fashioned wardrobe. Wearing only my bra and half slip, I fell onto the bed and almost instantly slept.

When I awoke, the light in the room was much dimmer. I turned on the bedside lamp, a ceramic horror in the shape of a mermaid holding a red rayon shade, and looked at my watch. Almost seven. Surely Jim had returned to his hotel room by now. I lifted the phone and gave the woman at the desk the International's number.

Jim was still out.

I hung up and lay back on the bed in the lamp's ruddy glow. Now that I was somewhat rested, I became aware that my last meal had been coffee and Danish, aboard the plane twelve hours before. Well, if I were to remedy that hollowness in my stomach,

54

I would have to risk going out to a restaurant. The Briault offered only Continental breakfasts, served either in one's room or at a plastic-topped table near the TV set in the dismal little lounge. I showered and then dressed in the coolest clothing my suitcase held —a brown skirt of some wool-and-synthetic material, and a sleeveless white silk jersey with a turtle neck. After I had hung the rest of my clothing in the wardrobe, I went downstairs.

The brunette was still on duty. "Forgive me, mademoiselle," she said, as I laid my key on the desk. "I forgot to tell you when you made your call a few minutes ago, but a gentleman called you around five o'clock. I told him you were not to be disturbed."

"That's all right." I preferred anyway to talk to Eric from the lobby phone booth, so that there would be no possibility of her listening in.

When I had closed the door of the booth near the foot of the stairs, I took from my shoulder bag the number he had written down for me. He answered on the first ring. I said, "Are you all right? Have have the police or anyone been there?"

"No one. How about you? Did you get some sleep?"

"Several hours. I'm going out to dinner now. After that I'll call the International again. I still have been able to get in touch with Jim."

"Let me know as soon as you do. I'll be right here Enjoy your dinner, honey."

I left the booth, nodded to the brunette, and went out into the lingering daylight. There was no need prices in the window looked a little cheaper than the other places around here. At least I think they did. I haven't gotten the hang of French money yet. You mind if I join you?"

I tried to sound cordial. "Please do."

She placed her handbag, a large one of brown plastic, on the table and sat down. "What's that you're having?"

"Veal stew. It's good."

She turned to the waitress. "I'll have the same."

"Pardón, madame?"

I said to the waitress, *"Le ragoût de veau, s'il vous plaît."*

When the waitress had turned away, my companion said, "It must be great to speak French."

"It comes in handy. How is your hotel?"

"Oh, it's nice. Real French, you know, with a bee-day in the bathroom. Of course, the lift is sort of small."

The lift. Perhaps she felt that the English term for elevator, like her Eiffel Tower bracelet, lent her that well-traveled touch. "Are you enjoying Paris?"

"Oh, yes. I slept two hours, and then I took the rubberneck tour, and then I did the Louvre, and Napoleon's Tomb."

"All in one afternoon?"

"Yes. I wanted to see as much as I could." Her voice went flat. "Mother's cablegram was waiting for me at the hotel. Aunt May—she lives with us, moved into our apartment two years ago after Uncle Joe died—Aunt May has to go into the hospital Thursday.

It was real sudden. Her doctor says she has to have tests. Mother wants me to fly home Wednesday. She's too nervous to be alone at night, what with all these robberies we've been having in Queens."

So, not Brooklyn, after all. I wondered about Mother. If Aunt May's health had remained robust, would Mother have found some other reason to summon Daughter home? "I'm awfully sorry you won't have your two weeks in Paris."

"Well, that's life. And anyway," she said, brightening somewhat, "while my aunt's in the hospital, I can have her twin bed in the bedroom. I won't have to sleep on the Castro convertible. Say, what's your name?"

"Dorothy. Dorothy Wanger."

"Pleased to meet you, Dorothy." She extended her hand across the table, and I, feeling like a fool, shook it. "My name's Rose. Rose Quinn."

Rose. I looked at the lumpy face, no doubt swarthy-skinned beneath its liquid makeup. Why did parents tempt Fate, that inveterate practical joker, by naming their girl children Rose, or Lily, or Violet?

Her ragout arrived. After a moment she said, "My, that is good." She laid down her fork. "Say, maybe we should have wine with our dinner, this being Paris and all. It'll be my treat."

"No, let me." For the price of wine, she could buy some additional souvenir of her sadly curtailed stay in Paris.

"Well, let's go Dutch."

With that settled, I ordered a carafe of *vin or-*

58

dinaire, and filled our glasses. "Cheers!" Rose said, lifting her glass, and I responded, "Cheers."

A moment later I asked, "Do you have brothers and sisters?"

"No, I wish I did. Then maybe Mother—How about you?"

"A sister. And a much older half-sister and a half-brother."

The anxiety the thought of Judson brought me must have shown in my face, because she asked, "What's the matter? Some of your folks sick?"

"Not really. It's just that my brother seems—disturbed."

"You mean you think he's nuts?"

I wished I had not brought up the subject of brothers and sisters. "Not exactly. But he's always been rather eccentric. And the last time I saw him, he said some strange things. But then, maybe I misunderstood him."

"Sure, that's probably it. People are always getting their wires crossed."

I said, eager to close the subject, "Well, I'm not going to keep on worrying about it. I intend to call him up the minute I get back to New York, and demand that he explain the whole thing to me."

"You do that, honey. There's nothing like putting your mind at rest, especially if all it takes is a phone call." She paused. "Say, do you know something? I was surprised to see you in here alone. I'd have expected you to be out with some man." When I did not answer, she said, "Excuse me. Maybe I shouldn't have said that. I mean, maybe you've got a husband back in New York."

"I'm not married. Not now." With chagrin I realized that nerve strain had made me unnecessarily talkative. I need not have added, "Not now."

"Divorced, huh? He must have been a real wrongo to make a nice girl like you get rid of him. It's funny how people fall for the wrong people, isn't it?"

"Yes." Turning the stem of my glass, I thought of a cocktail party more than a year before in an eighth-floor suite of a Madison Avenue hotel. Natalie, in town for a series of TV appearances to promote her latest film, was giving the party. I found myself standing on the fringes of a small crowd which, wherever she moved in the flower-filled, softly lighted room, seemed to form around her. Of course the crowd was composed mainly of men. As I looked at her standing there, red hair brushing the shoulders of a black velvet dress primly long-sleeved and high-necked in front, but cut two inches below the waist in back, the inevitable metaphor came to mind. She was the flame, surrounded by fatuously smiling moths.

One of the moths, a lanky blond man with horn-rimmed spectacles, turned away from the circle so quickly that he sent the glass in my hand rolling away over the dark green wall-to-wall carpet. "Oh, Lord!" he said. "What was it? A martini?"

He mopped at the rug with his handkerchief, took my empty glass to the bar, and came back with a filled one. "I'm awfully sorry."

We introduced ourselves. He said, "Wanger?" He

60

turned to look at the group surrounding Natalie. "Any relation to that unbelievably gorgeous—"

"I'm her sister."

"Her sister! Why, you don't look anything like her!" Appalled color dyed his face. "Oh, Lord! I didn't mean it that way. You're pretty too. You're awfully pretty. It's just that you're so much shorter, and your hair is blond, and—"

"Don't strain yourself." My tone was dry, but I really didn't feel annoyed. I was used to seeing incredulity in people's faces when they learned I was Natalie's sister. And I liked him for that appalled look. Here was someone genuinely reluctant to give pain.

"Should I get us some stuff from the buffet? We could sit over there against the wall and talk."

We did. I told him about my job. He told me about his, and that he had come to the party with a friend —a TV producer. At last he asked me to go to dinner with him.

I said, standing up, "I'll say good-bye to Natalie."

When, at my signal, she left a group of guests and walked over to me, I said, "Lovely party. I'm leaving now. Someone's taking me to dinner."

"Who?"

"The one getting into his raincoat over there by the door."

"Oh, Eric Lang." So she had taken sufficient notice of him to remember his name. "Well, I had put him on my reserve list, but no matter." She kissed my forehead. "Have a good time, sweetie."

I knew what she meant by her reserve list. Natalie led a love life as untrammeled and lighthearted as that of any man.

Eric and I descended in an elevator to Madison Avenue, where the pavement, wet with March rain, gave back the smeared reflection of green and blue and red neon lights. Before that evening was over, I knew I could fall in love with him. Yes, even though he took someone else's raincoat from the rack in the small Italian restaurant where we dined, and we had to go back for his own. And yes, even though he spent a large part of the evening, both in the restaurant and the Third Avenue bar we later visited, asking me questions about Natalie.

I had feared I would not see him again. But when I landed at Kennedy after my next flight, and drove my VW to my East Eighty-seventh Street apartment, I found his note waiting for me. Some Vermont friends of his had asked him for a skiing weekend. Would I go with him? He scarcely mentioned Natalie that weekend, or on subsequent dates. Soon I was sure that his feeling for her had been about as important as a crush he might have had on Gina Lollobrigida, say, at the age of fourteen.

In early May he asked me to marry him. By that time I was so much in love that if he hadn't proposed, I probably would have.

Rose said, "Excuse me if I'm getting out of line, but what was the trouble between you and your ex? Another girl?"

"Please, Rose. If you don't mind, I'd rather not talk about it."

"Oh, sure, honey!" She paused for a moment, and then went on, "I told you I was on the rubberneck bus today, didn't I? Well, I sat next to this lady from Kansas City, and she said, 'Didn't you wrap a package for me once at Abraham and Straus?' And I said, 'I sure might have. I work at the wrapping desk. When were you at A and S?'"

Her voice went on and on. And on. I made some sort of response now and then, but I really was not listening. In my thoughts I was not even there, in a Paris restaurant growing rapidly more crowded. I had returned to the cottage, perched on the dunes above a Bridgehampton Beach, far out on eastern Long Island, which Eric and I had rented for three weeks the previous August. I remembered how, just as I climbed the steps from the beach after a midmorning swim our first Saturday there, the phone had rung. With sand gritting under my bare feet, I crossed the small living room to answer it.

It was Natalie calling from less than ten miles away. She had flown to New York to be on the Today show. Afterwards, she had accepted the invitation of a network executive, someone named Claybuck, to spend the weekend at the Claybucks' Southampton place.

"I had no idea what I was letting myself in for. All the other guests are well into their Golden Years. At dinner last night we discussed arthritis and grandchildren. This morning the more ambulatory guests are knocking croquet balls around on the south lawn, and the rest are cheering them on from the terrace.

63

backgammon."

I knew that this was one of Natalie's hyperbolic moods. Probably the truth was merely that the house party included no one both attractive and available. But as always, her exaggerations amused me.

"We've got an extra bedroom. Think you could cut out for the rest of the weekend?"

"Like a shot. There's a fleet of cars in the garage here. If I can't borrow one, I'll steal it. Around five okay?"

"Fine. We'll take you on a beach picnic some Amagansett friends are giving." I smiled, thinking of how dazzled Jill and Lonnie Winston would be when we drove up to the picnic site with Natalie.

I hung up and turned to see Eric standing there in his swim trunks. "Natalie's coming for the rest of the weekend."

Toweling his hair, he frowned. "From what I've seen of her, I don't think she'll fit in on a picnic."

I had long since forgiven Eric for talking so much about Natalie on our first date. Nevertheless, I was pleased that he seemed not in the least eager to see her now. "She'll fit in fine. The Winstons will be talking for months about how they shared burned steak and sandy corn on the cob with Natalie Wanger."

I made up the bed for Natalie in the smaller of the two bedrooms. Eric and I were eating an early lunch off a card table in the living room when again the telephone rang. This time it was Marv Sayers, of Columbia Flight Personnel. "Dottie, I hate like hell to

64

ask this of you, but could you drive here to Kennedy right away? There's a special charter flight, Los Angeles to Paris by way of New York, due in here at seven o'clock. We're short two stewardesses for the New York to Paris leg."

"No!" I said, wishing Eric and I had chosen Nova Scotia or some equally remote spot for our vacation. "Absolutely not."

"Where's that old team spirit? Besides, it'll pay off. I'll wangle you an extra week's vacation, a full seven days."

An additional week out here on the dunes, plus extra flight pay. "All right. I'd better leave here soon, because I'll have to drive in to the apartment for my uniform."

When I hung up, I saw from the look on Eric's face that Marv had talked loudly enough for him to hear. "Hell," he said.

"I know. But think of it. After I get back we can stay out here until the end of the month. And we can use that extra money, too."

"I suppose so. You'd better call Natalie and tell her to stay put where she is."

I looked up the Claybucks' number. Before I lifted the phone, I said, "You go to the picnic and have a good time. The Winstons can drive over and pick you up. And I'll be back here by Tuesday, maybe earlier."

I dialed. When a thin, dry voice said, "Mr. and Mrs. Claybuck's residence," I asked, "May I speak to Miss Wanger?"

"Certainly, madam. But it may take me some time

to bring her to the telephone. She and the other guests are out somewhere on the grounds."

I pictured the owner of that elderly voice trying to make a quick search of one of those huge Southampton estates, moving with stiff gait from swimming pool to rose garden to guest cottages to tennis courts. "Please don't bother. Just have her call when she comes in." I gave him the number and hung up.

As I headed toward our bedroom to pack, I said to Eric, "You tell her what happened. Better stick close to the phone until she calls. I've got to get going."

When I walked into Marv's office about four hours later, the hangdog look on his face told me instantly that my battle with Expressway traffic, and my drive through Manhattan's potholed streets to my—now our—apartment, and then the drive back across the Triborough Bridge to Kennedy, had been an utter waste. "I'm sorry," he said. "It was a snafu all around."

He explained that in Los Angeles the charter passengers, all of them American Garden Club members, had waited an hour in the plane while mechanics tried in vain to stop a leak in the hydraulic system. Finally the passengers were transferred to another plane, which skidded on the runway and broke a wheel.

"No one was hurt, thank God, but they were so mad by then that we had to switch their flight to Pan Am."

He added placatingly, "I'll put through a time-and-expense voucher for you."

66

I smiled at him. After all, it wasn't his fault. "Do you think Columbia's generosity would run to a call to Bridgehampton?"

He shoved the phone toward me. "Be our guest."

As I expected, there was no answer. By now Eric would be picnicking with the Winstons on the sunset-dyed beach at Amagansett. What was more, he might stay there until close to midnight. I said good-bye to Marv and walked out through the terminal's familiar fluorescent glare.

I would stay the night at the apartment, I decided as I moved toward the parking lot, and drive out to the cottage early the next morning. In all, I had driven about a hundred and sixty miles that day. I did not relish the thought of an additional hundred and ten.

I reached the stiflingly hot apartment around eight. Even though we had closed the windows before we left it less than a week before, coal dust had seeped in to coat our new maple furniture. I turned on the only air conditioning unit, the one in the bedroom, and then dialed the Bridgehampton number. Apparently Eric was still at the picnic.

I opened a can of chicken noodle soup and ate all of it, thinking of how strange and depressing it seemed, after only a little more than three months of marriage, to be eating alone in the breakfast nook. Then I showered and went to bed.

By seven o'clock the next morning I had left the Grand Central Parkway and was on the Long Island Expressway, making good time through the blessedly truck-free traffic. Despite the gray overcast the air was oppressively hot. Soon after I crossed the Suffolk County line, though, light rain began to fall. I welcomed it, even though it forced me to reduce speed. In fact, I hoped the rain would grow heavier. After nearly a week of sunshine, it would be a pleasant novelty to sit with Eric on the cottage's tiny porch and watch rain fall on a deserted beach and gray ocean.

To the sound of church bells, I drove down Bridgehampton's elm-bordered Main Street. On the sidewalks only a few pedestrians, probably churchgoers, moved past the closed shops through the gray drizzle. I turned to my right, along a street of nineteenth-century houses set far back on wide lawns, and then struck across a dirt road that ran through blossoming potato fields toward the ocean.

Our own even narrower side road ended behind the dunes. All the previous week, from nine in the morning on, a line of cars had stood there while their owners swam or sun-bathed. Now there was only one car, a white station wagon with a Suffolk County license. Some local fisherman, out to try his luck undisturbed by the usual gawking, question-asking summer people. I parked the VW and climbed the sloping footpath to the beach.

The cottage's living room was empty. Quietly, so as not to disturb Eric, I crossed to the bedroom's partially opened door and looked in. This room, its bed neatly made, was also empty. Puzzled but not alarmed, I moved farther into the room. Had he gone out for a walk along the rainy beach? No, the smoothly made bed was proof that he had not slept in it the night before. Eric-made beds always looked like a relief map of the Appalachian foothills. He must have spent the night at the Winstons.

I went back into the living room and started toward the phone. Then I stopped and looked at the closed door of the other bedroom.

I looked at it for perhaps thirty seconds, thinking of the station wagon with the Suffolk license. Perhaps it was not a fisherman's. With a sick distaste for the picture which had formed in my mind, I moved to that door and quietly opened it.

As usual, Eric was sleeping on his stomach. He had pushed down the sheet on his side of the bed, so that his tanned back was naked from broad shoulders to narrow waist. Natalie lay on her back, sheet pulled up almost to her bare shoulders, one hand loosely curled beside the fan of red hair spread out on the pillow.

I stood motionless, feeling nothing at all. After a while, as if sensing my presence, Natalie opened her eyes. At first those great green eyes looked unfocused, clouded with sleep. Then I saw consternation leap into her face, and heard her swift intake of breath.

The sound seemed to release me. I turned and walked to the front door and down the steps. When I reached the beach, I began to run through the light drizzle, with the damp sand dragging at my feet. After fifty yards or so I stumbled over something, perhaps a half-buried log, and fell to my hands and knees. It seemed too much trouble to stand up, so I just sat on the sand, looking out over the water.

I still had that strange emptiness of feeling. The sensation was familiar, and after a moment I identified it. I had felt this way when I first learned of my parents' sudden death. No wonder I had the feeling again, because there had been another sudden death. Death of trust, and shared laughter, and lightheartedness. Death of a marriage.

I still sat there, wondering vaguely when the numbness would wear off and grief would tear at me. A few feet away, sandpipers skittered on stilt legs, pecking at tiny creatures left by each wave's ebb, and then retreating before the next wave's advance. Farther out gulls circled and dove with harsh cries, their bodies white against the gray sky and darker gray water.

Someone was moving toward me along the beach. I turned my head long enough to see that it was Natalie in black pants and an emerald green jersey, with a black suede bag slung over her shoulder. Then I turned my gaze back to the water.

She came and stood in front of me. "Oh, Dottie! Oh, your little face! Listen to me. Listen to me, baby."

To my surprise, I found that I could speak. "Was Eric afraid to come out here? Is that why he sent you?"

"Darling, no! I persuaded him it would be best if I talked to you first."

"When you called him yesterday, did he tell you that the coast would be clear for several days?" How was it, I wondered, that I could sound so calm?

"You've got it all wrong!" I saw her slender hand tighten around the shoulder bag's strap. "I didn't phone yesterday. That senile fool of a butler forgot to give me the message. I drove over here around five yesterday afternoon. The Winstons were here. They'd come to pick up Eric, and they asked me to come to the picnic, too."

She stopped speaking. With no desire to help her out, I remained silent. At last she went on, "Around midnight, they brought us both back here, so that I could pick up the Claybucks' station wagon. Eric and I decided to have a nightcap. And then . . . Oh, Dottie. Eric loves you. None of this was his fault."

I still spoke in that calm voice, as if she and I were discussing the weather. "Sure. You lassoed him and dragged him into the bedroom."

"Darling, darling! You don't have to lasso a man. All you have to do is to make him feel that if he turns you down you'll think that he's a boor, or that maybe he's not quite . . . Oh, Dottie! Please! Believe it or not, I love you too."

I looked at my beautiful sister, thinking of how warm and generous she had been in the past, helping me choose clothes during our teens, and showing pride in my few accomplishments, such as my editorship of the high school paper. Later on, she had flown from the west coast to the east and back within twenty-four hours, just so that she could sit applauding when I received my college diploma.

And yet, as casually as she might have torn up an old letter, she had destroyed the only happiness I might ever have with a man. "If you love me, why did you stay here last night?"

She said, with Natalie-like simplicity, "Because I had no idea you'd ever find out. If you hadn't, what harm would there have been?"

That was one of the silly self-justifications people made. Of course there would have been harm. Those hours he had spent with Natalie could not have helped but affect Eric's feeling for me, whether or not I was ever aware of what had happened.

She said in a flat voice, "I don't suppose it's any use to tell you how sorry I am, or to ask you to forgive me."

Perhaps I would find I could forgive her forty or fifty years from now.

For a while there was no sound except the gulls' cries and the break and withdrawing seethe of waves. Then she said, "I'd better get back to the Claybucks'. I'll be there until four, if you want to phone me."

I watched her move up to the beach toward the break in the dunes which marked the road. When she had disappeared, I stood up, automatically brushed damp sand from my clothing, and started toward the cottage. Halfway there I saw Eric walking toward me in old blue jeans and a striped jersey.

He stopped in front of me. "Don't look like that," he said. "Is there anything I can do to stop you looking like that?" He pointed toward the water. "Shall I go out there and just keep swimming? Would that do it?"

Afterwards I often wondered what would have happened if I had said yes. But I said nothing at all. I moved past him toward the steps. He kept pace with me. In the living room I picked up my suitcase, carried it into the bedroom, and opened it on the bed. I was aware of him leaning against the door jamb, his face so white it looked muddy through its tan. "What are you doing?"

I carried a pile of underclothing from the bureau to the suitcase before I replied. "I'm going to the apartment. I'll pack your things and send them down here if you want."

"I love you. Please don't leave me. I don't want you to leave me."

Probably he didn't. He knew that last night had not increased his chances one whit for anything permanent with Natalie. For her, love was not just a sometime thing. It often was a one-time thing. And so he wanted to hang onto good old Dottie—square, reliable old Dottie.

I took more clothing from the bureau. "I am leaving you. Where shall I send your things? To the Bridgehampton post office?"

After a while he said dully, "Send them to the NYU Club. I won't stay down here alone."

In New York on Monday, I asked for, and received, a leave of absence from my job. Two days later I flew to Nevada for a six weeks' stay at a dude ranch which catered to prospective divorcées near Las Vegas. I was in a pretty bad way. At one point I even tried to work up an interest in one of the ersatz cowboys which the management provided for us casualties from the marital battlefields.

I felt much calmer after I returned to work. I began to date Jim Henderson and other men in New York and Paris. Perhaps if Eric had not begun to turn up on my flights, by now I might have been ready to fall in love with someone else.

"—best place to buy gloves?"

With a start I realized that Rose Quinn had paused in her monologue to ask a question. "Gloves?"

"For Mother and Aunt May. Where's the best place to buy them?"

"Better to go to one of the big department stores. Gloves from the tourist traps may turn stiff as a board if they get wet, and the smart shops are too expensive." I saw that her wineglass was empty. I filled her glass, added a little to my own, and then looked at my watch. Nearly eight. "Will you excuse me? I have to make a phone call."

In the telephone booth near the kitchen doorway I learned that Jim Henderson still had not picked up his hotel room key. Perhaps, I reflected as I hung up, he would spend the night somewhere else. And since I had never looked into his little black book, I had no idea where that place might be.

For a moment I thought of trying to phone Mimi. Perhaps she might have some idea of how I could find Jim. But no, she would start asking questions. As

74

for my not turning up at the hotel tonight, that would not worry her. When she had last seen me there at the bus terminal, Eric had been walking toward me. With her romantic turn of mind she would assume that, in her phrase, we had gotten back together.

Besides, I thought, feeling my hands turn cold, if that outraged commissaire had sent a policeman to the International, he might have questioned my roommate and asked her to notify the police if she heard from me. I couldn't risk plunging her into a conflict between friendship and duty by calling her.

When I returned to the table, Rose looked at me eagerly through her pink-rimmed glasses. "Say, I've been thinking. Since you don't have a date, and I don't either— I mean, is it okay for girls to go to night clubs in Paris?"

"As far as I know, there's no law against it."

"Do you think we could afford the Lido?"

"At eighty francs for a floor show and a bottle of fourth-rate champagne? No. Besides, I need sleep."

She said in a subdued voice, "I suppose I'd be pretty conspicuous going someplace like that alone."

She certainly would. I thought of mentioning the Robert Redford picture at the cinema next to Le Drugstore. But it would have seemed heartless to suggest that she spend her first night in Paris—her first of only two nights—at a movie, particularly a movie she could see in her own Queens neighborhood.

"Paris has a lot more than night life to offer," I said. "Why don't you go to your hotel now, get up early, and take the boat trip along the Seine in the morning and the Versailles tour in the afternoon? You wouldn't want to go home without seeing Versailles, would you?"

"No," she said, but she still seemed depressed, which—given Mother, and the one-bedroom apartment in Queens, and her imminent return to both— I could well understand. And so, after the waitress had brought our coffee, I said, "What flight are you taking on Wednesday?"

"I don't know. I haven't made my reservation. The desk clerk at my hotel said there'd be plenty of seats, midweek like that."

Perhaps, too, she had wanted to postpone the moment of canceling nearly all of the vacation she had been planning for months, perhaps years. "Why don't you take the three o'clock? I'll be on that flight." At least, I thought grimly, I hoped I would be.

She brightened. "You will? I'd been meaning to ask when you were flying back to New York. All right. I'll try for the three o'clock. I'll call the airline as soon as I get back to the hotel."

When our checks came, she gave me two-francs-eighty for her half of the wine. We paid the woman at the high cashier's desk and went out into the now dark street.

"I'll walk with you as far as the corner," I said. "I want to buy something before I go back to my hotel." Tired as I was, I did not feel drowsy. Perhaps the paperback department at Le Drugstore, which carried books in French and English ranging from

Shakespeare to Camus to Jacqueline Sussann, would have *A Key to "Finnegans Wake."*

At the corner I looked after her for a moment as, long skirt swaying from ample hips, she crossed Boulevard St.-Germain. Then I turned to my right along the broad sidewalk.

Chapter 6

LE Drugstore's curving aisles were jammed with shoppers buying perfume, wine, floppy-brimmed hats, and even drugs. I eeled my way past small stands displaying boxed incense, potted cacti, and sunglasses, and descended steps to the book alcove.

No *Key*. Perhaps Eric was right. Perhaps I should give up on Joyce.

I had ascended the steps, and was moving toward the store's entrance, when I felt something prick my bare left arm. Startled, I turned. A man of about forty stood there holding a tiny barrel cactus in one hand.

"I regret, mademoiselle! Did I—"

"It's all right," I said, rubbing the spot. "It didn't really hurt."

I left Le Drugstore and moved through the side-walk crowd. I had almost reached Rue des Saints-Pères when, as had happened earlier that day, weariness overwhelmed me like a wave. But it was worse now. I felt nauseous and slightly dizzy. Bed, I thought. I was too tired even to make another no-doubt futile phone call to the International. I turned the corner and went down the side street, so unsteady with fatigue that I brushed against one of the cars parked with left-hand wheels up on the curb.

The brunette behind the hotel desk had been replaced by a stooped gray-haired night clerk. He gave me my key. In my room I stripped, put on a nightgown, hung my skirt and sleeveless turtleneck in the wardrobe, and tumbled into bed.

I dreamed. Eric and I were at Bridgehampton, swimming side by side through still water beyond the last line of waves, and we were happy. Then we began to quarrel fiercely—it was something about my sister—and he turned and began to swim toward the horizon. Numb with terror, I tried to call for him to come back. I could not. Soon he turned anyway, and I, heart swelling with joy, swam to meet him.

The scene changed. Natalie, standing beside me at a dressing table, was smoothing green shadow onto my eyelids. She wore jeans and a cable-knit sweater I remembered from her twentieth year and my own eighteenth. "Yes, I like men," she said. "But one thing, honey. I'll never even look at any man of yours." I was about to say, "I know you won't," but before I could say it, my dreaming self was back in the hotel room and Gastand was there too, along with a slender blond girl of about twenty-three who smiled at me pleasantly in the lamp's red glow. "Get up, Dorothy. We're going out." Of course, I thought, and got out of bed.

She was very helpful. She led me into the bathroom, brought me my blue sweater and Madras pants and my shoulder bag, and helped me dress. I felt I had seen her before, but I did not know where. Then she and Gastand and I were out in the hall. I thought of telling them that the elevator was too small for three people, but evidently they knew that, because we were going down the stairs. "Leave your key," the girl said. The desk clerk smiled broadly as I laid my key on the desk, and someone—I don't think it was I—said good night to him.

We were in a car, with Gastand driving, and the girl beside me in the back seat. I saw the reflection of bridge lights in the Seine and, an unmeasured interval later, the Egyptian monolith in the Place de la Concorde. It seemed to sway against the night sky as I looked at it, but somehow that did not bother me. Where were we going? To a party far out on the Champs Élysées, or in Passy?

Without remembering how I got there, I was in a big room with smoked mirrors on the walls. I had a vague impression of luxurious bad taste—sofas and armchairs upholstered in black leather, and lots of mirror-top tables holding small statuary. Gastand and the girl were still in the dream, and so was another man, tall and thin and bald, with rimless glasses.

"All right, girls," the bald man said in French. "Stand here."

I stood beside her. I could see us in one of the smoked mirrors, and now I knew why I thought I had seen her before. She looked very much like me.

The bald man said, "There's about a half-inch difference in height." A muscle at the corner of his mouth twitched. A second later, it twitched again. I watched it, fascinated.

"A half-inch won't matter. Anyway, she can wear inner soles."

She? I decided they meant the other girl. I could see she was a little shorter than I was.

"The eyes aren't the same shade," the bald man went on.

"Dark glasses. Or, if you want to get fancy, contact lenses."

"The hair will have to be shortened, and the nose isn't quite—"

"That can be fixed at the last minute. Everything can be fixed."

The bald man's voice was cold. "Let's hope so." The muscle was twitching faster now. "But I realize more than ever what an idiotic stunt you tried to pull this morning."

"I think my way would have worked." Gastand sounded sullen.

"And I know it would not have. I think your success in finding this girl has gone to your head."

What girl? I decided that they meant me. They went on quarreling. I listened placidly, not caring that their voices had begun to fade in and out, so that I could not even hear all that they said, let alone know what the trouble was.

"If you really wanted to play safe," Gastand said. His voice faded and then sounded loud again, like a radio when the transistor is about to go out. "—handle everything from the New York end."

"I can't go to New York. I'm here, and so everything will be run from here. Everything, every step of the way." The bald man's voice also faded. "—got that straight?"

Gastand didn't answer. The bald man reached over to a table and picked up a camera that hadn't been in the dream before. A flash dazzled my eyes. At his direction, the other girl and I turned our heads first to the right, and then the left. There were more flashes. With placid amusement, I thought of how we were like Mimi and me going through the same motions of the life-jacket routine.

The bald man said pleasantly, "Sit down, Dorothy. No, not there," as I moved toward a sofa, "over there."

I sat down in a deep, soft leather armchair. I heard a click, and saw that he had turned on a tape recorder which rested on a table beside me. He said, in English now, "Say, 'See you later.' "

"See you later."

"Say, 'Hi, there. Let me in.' "

"Hi, there. Let me in."

"Not like that. More eagerly. You want to see this person. Now say it."

"Hi, there. Let me in. Hi, there. Let me in. Hi, there—"

He laughed. "That's enough. Now say, 'I'm dying for a cup of coffee.' Say it as if you really wanted coffee."

The dream grew blurred. He told me to say more things. Then Gastand and the girl and I were in the car again. The bald man was not with us. We turned onto a narrow street where cars stood oddly slanted. Rue des Saints-Pères? "Ask for your key," the girl said.

After the dark outside, the light in the cramped lobby hurt my eyes. I said, "My key, if you please, monsieur." In the dream I was aware that the old desk clerk, not smiling now, looked at me with troubled eyes as he handed me my key.

It was Gastand who unlocked my door. He opened the flap of my shoulder bag and dropped the key inside. "Good night, Dorothy," he said. "Go back to bed."

Chapter 7

$\blacktriangleleft\!\!\!\!\!\blacktriangleleft\!\!\!\!\!\blacktriangleleft\!\!\!\!\!\blacktriangleleft\!\!\!\!\!\blacktriangleleft$

As one sometimes does after a sleep crowded with dreams, I awoke feeling almost as tired as when I had gone to bed. I looked at my watch—ten past eight—and then lay back, looking at the faded wallpaper, and wondering what Dr. Jens, my college psychology professor, would have said about the antics of my dreaming self. Not, I thought wryly, that the swimming-with-Eric dream would offer a Freudian interpreter any difficulty. And anyway, all these months I had been aware of how much I missed Eric's lovemaking. The wish-fulfillment basis of the Natalie dream was equally obvious. My dreaming self had wanted to wipe out, not just the reality of what I had seen from a bedroom doorway that drizzly morning in Bridgehampton; it had wanted to pretend that Eric and Natalie simply could not have turned to each other, ever.

It was the Gastand dream that disturbed me. Not that it had been a frightening dream. I had gone with him willingly, and nothing unpleasant, let alone terrifying, had happened to me. In fact, it was that very lack of nightmare quality which disturbed me.

After a moment, feeling chilled, I realized why the pleasant tone of the dream so troubled me. Had I, in some recess of my unconscious, *wanted* yesterday to get into Gastand's dark green car, just as my dreaming self had gotten into that car with him and the blond girl? And that girl. A Freudian might say that in the dream I looked like Gastand's girl companion because I wished to be her.

But that would mean I was really sick. Sick enough to imagine yesterday that a handsome, well-dressed stranger had tried to force me into his car. Sick enough that, in reality, I might have tried to pick him up, just as he had reported to that commissaire.

No! I was not crazy. I had never been even—peculiar, like my half-brother. Always I had regarded myself as too normal, too average. Others saw me that way, too. I recalled that once Natalie had said, with a shake of her head, "Dottie, if you'd been born in Iowa you'd have been recording secretary of your 4-H Club."

To hell with the dream, and to hell with Freud. I had imagined nothing yesterday. Gastand's words had been real, and so had the gun in his pocket. And what I needed was not help from a shrink, but from Jim Henderson.

I reached for the phone. The woman desk clerk was back on duty. I gave her the International's number.

Monsieur Henderson still had not picked up his room key.

Useless to wonder bitterly in whose flat he lay sleeping or sat enjoying breakfast. Best to go downstairs for my own breakfast. If my stay at this hotel eight years before was any criterion, coffee I ordered to my room would arrive lukewarm. And once I'd had coffee, I would call Eric. Perhaps we could think of someone besides Jim to go to bat for us. I got out of bed, went to the wardrobe, and took down the skirt and the turtleneck jersey I had worn the night before.

It was not until I turned away from the wardrobe that I saw it—that tangle of clothing there on the floor beside the bed. Bra, pantyhose, and the green sweater and madras pants that girl in the dream had helped me put on.

Throat dry and knees weak, I sank onto the room's one chair, a straight one upholstered in worn red plush. I stared at the heap of garments on the floor. To my conscious recollection, the last time I had worn those pants and that sweater had been two weeks before in New York.

Did it mean that the dream had been real?

Or did it mean that sometime during the night I had gotten up, dressed, and wandered along through the Paris streets, all the time hallucinating about Gastand, and a girl, and a room with dark mirrors, and a bald man with a tick?

For a moment I felt paralyzed by what must be among the worst of terrors, the fear that one has lost the ability to distinguish real events from imagined ones, and solid bodies from phantoms. Then I began to struggle against that fear. Surely there was some way to find out what had happened last night.

The old desk clerk. I remembered how in the dream his face had worn an almost conspiratorial smile when my companions and I left the hotel, and a troubled look when—how many minutes or hours later?—I had asked him for my room key. Surely he could tell me whether I had come down to the lobby alone last night, or with a man and a girl, or not at all. It would be embarrassing to ask such a question. But better any amount of embarrassment than the bewilderment and self-doubt I now felt.

I dressed in the skirt and turtleneck as swiftly as my unsteady hands could manage. Because the air coming in the open window was cooler than that of yesterday, I added a white cardigan of thin wool. Then I picked up my shoulder bag, went out into the hall, and, after locking my door, descended the stairs.

The woman at the desk had sounded calm and pleasant when I asked to be connected with the International. Now, looking harassed, she was speaking into the phone in rapid French. "—early this morning. Send someone experienced if you can." She hung up and said to me, "Good morning, mademoiselle. You would like your breakfast served in the lounge?"

"Yes, please. But first, does your night clerk have a room here in the hotel?"

Her expression altered. "No."

"Then could you tell me where I might find him?"

"You can't, mademoiselle. He is dead. He was

struck by a car as he was going home early this morning."

I clutched the desk's raised edge. "A car?"

"Yes. The driver must have lost control. It came up on the sidewalk on the Rue St. Guill—poor old Armand and his wife had an apartment there—and crushed him against a building. Then it went on."

"Did anyone see—"

"Only a taxi driver, and he was at least a hundred feet away. It happened a little past five in the morning, when it was still almost dark. Of late years I have allowed Armand to go home two hours earlier than he used to. One of the porters takes over the desk until I— What is it, mademoiselle? Were you acquainted with Armand Dubois?"

"No." Not a coincidence, I was thinking; surely not a coincidence.

"Why is it you wanted to see him? Perhaps I can help you."

Her gaze had sharpened. Don't talk to her about it, I warned myself. Don't talk to anyone until you've seen Eric. "Thank you, but it was nothing important."

After a moment she said, "Very well. If you will go into the lounge, I will send someone to take your breakfast order."

"Thank you. But first I must make a call."

I went into the booth and with shaking fingers felt in the side pocket of my shoulder bag. The slip of paper which bore Eric's phone number was still there.

Again he must have been very near the phone,

because he answered on the first ring. "Eric, I must see you."

Instantly his voice became alarmed. "What is it?"

"I've got to see you, that's all." My voice rose. "Right away."

"Sure, honey." He spoke swiftly, soothingly. "I'll be there as soon as I can."

"No!" I felt an overwhelming need to be away from the curious eyes of the woman watching me through the booth's glass door, away from this ordinary little hotel which for me had become shadowy and sinister.

After a moment he said, "It'll be quicker if we meet at some halfway point. You know that little café on the north side of the Place des Vosges?"

"Yes."

"I'll be there in twenty minutes."

I hung up and left the booth. The woman behind the desk said, "Forgive me, but you seem upset. Did something happen here last night?"

Despite her polite tone, there was cold suspicion in her eyes. Was she really wondering if something had happened? Or was she wondering how much I remembered?

The thought was absurd, I instantly realized. It was only natural for her to wonder about why I seemed upset. Nevertheless, that look in her eyes made me want more than ever to get away from this place, clear away.

"Nothing is wrong, madame. It is just that I find I must leave. Will you please make up my bill?"

Chapter 8

I WAS halfway down the steps of the Metro's St.-Germain station before full realization struck me.

That girl. Those men were grooming her to take my place.

I halted so abruptly that a woman descending the steps behind me struck my shoulder with hers. She gave me an indignant look and then went on down the steps. I still stood there, one hand clutching the handle of my suitcase, the other the rail.

Where was that girl now? Perhaps in the room with the smoked mirrors. Wherever she was, probably right now she was listening to that taped recording of my drugged voice. I imagined her repeating those phrases over and over again, until the irritable man with the tic gave a satisfied nod.

And when he was satisfied with her voice, and when the differences in her appearance from mine were corrected—height, hair length, eye color—when all that was accomplished, what would they do with *me?*

Get to Eric, I thought; get to Eric. I went on down the steps.

The morning rush hour was over. Only a few people sat on benches or sauntered up and down the platform. I stood as close as I could to the tunnel wall.

Fear is like a distorting lens. Even the light down there was not just murky and unpleasant, but sinister. Reason told me that those respectable-looking matrons were bound for the Right Bank department stores, and that those three sniggering youths near the platform's edge were probably messengers. As for the men in business suits, some of them carrying briefcases, probably they were just what they seemed to be—lawyers on their way to court, or bank representatives about to visit a wealthy client, or salesmen making calls on prospects. And yet something in me was convinced that if I ventured to the platform's edge, one of those prosaic-looking figures would slip up swiftly behind me and jostle me hard enough to send me plunging to the tracks.

A breeze stirred the hair on my damp forehead. One of those almost silent trains was pushing cool air ahead of it down the tunnel. I waited until it had stopped before I crossed the platform to board it.

Minutes later, in the sparsely filled car, I suddenly realized the absurdity of my fear back there in the station. If those two men and that girl had intended to kill me, they could have done so last night. They need never have brought me back to the Briault.

That terrible self-doubt returned. The very fact that I was alive and physically unharmed seemed to me evidence that if I had left the hotel at all the night before, it had been in the company of my own phantoms.

I transferred to another sparsely filled train. At a Right Bank stop I got off and climbed steps to clear, cool sunlight. When I had turned several corners, there ahead was the Place des Vosges, with tall old houses, their once-bright façades faded but still beautiful, rising on four sides of the square.

At this early hour, Eric was the only occupant of the sidewalk tables set out on the square's northern side. At sight of me he got up and hurried forward. He asked no questions as he took my suitcase from me, but I could tell by his face that my appearance alarmed him.

When we had sat down at his table, he signaled the waiter and ordered two coffees. As soon as the little cups were served and the waiter had moved away, Eric asked, "What is it?"

I told him.

When I had finished, I said, "Do you think I've gone crazy, Eric? Do you?"

His reply was not a hasty "No!" as it had been the day before. He said quietly, "We have to face the possibility. Such things happen. But I don't think it has happened to you. I think Gastand and that girl really did come to your room last night."

My eyes stung. I turned my face away. A bonneted and beplumed marble Louis the Thirteenth, out there in the square astride his marble battle charger, seemed to waver before my tear-blurred eyes. Nothing is lonelier than the fear of insanity. By admitting its possibility, Eric had shared that loneliness. By denying its probability, he had dissipated much of the fear.

"You must have been higher than a kite," he said. I turned my gaze back to him. "Now let's go over it again. That man in Le Drugstore, the one who pricked your arm with what you thought was a cactus. Did he look like either of the men in the back seat of the Ford?"

"I suppose so. But thousands of Frenchmen are dark-haired and fortyish and medium tall." What sort of drug, I wondered, had been used? Probably one of the hallucinogens, perhaps combined with sodium pentothal.

"Do you have any idea how Gastand knew you'd gone to the Briault? I was almost certain that if anyone was following us on the subway yesterday, we'd managed to shake them."

"No, I've no idea, unless . . . Eric! Did you telephone me at the hotel late yesterday afternoon?"

"Of course not. You'd told me you were going to sleep, so I waited until you called me."

"Someone phoned. The woman at the desk told me so when I came down to the lobby around seven last evening. I just assumed it had been you, and so I called you back."

"The telephone. So that's how they did it."

We sat in silence. I thought of Gastand and his companions, each with a telephone, and a partial list of Paris hotels. How many hotels had been called before the woman at the Briault said, "Yes, monsieur. Mademoiselle Dorothy Wanger is registered here, but she has asked not to be disturbed." If they had divided up the list alphabetically, the man calling hotels listed under the letters A through F, say, might have reached the Briault within an hour or less.

Eric said, "Do you have any idea what time it was when Gastand and the girl came to your room?"

"No."

"Do you think you let them in?"

"No. They were just there." I thought of the blond girl smiling down at me through the lamp's red glow.

"Do you think the night clerk was bribed to let them in, or to give them his passkey?"

I recalled the old man's gentle, respectable face. "I don't think he would have done that. I think they told him that the girl was my sister. He would have believed that. Anyone would have." I thought of the conspiratorial smile on the clerk's face when those two led me down to the lobby. "I think they'd told him they wanted to surprise me."

"And so he didn't ring your room. He just let them go up."

I nodded. "Maybe they knocked and I let them in, although I don't remember it that way. Probably they let themselves in. There don't seem to be any Yale locks at the Briault, just the old-fashioned kind. If they had brought several skeleton keys, one would have been almost sure to fit."

"Do you have any idea where they took you?"

"No, there were—gaps. I just know that at least for

a time the car was headed west. I remember passing the Place de la Concorde." I thought of my drugged self, placidly watching the monolith sway against the night sky.

"And when they brought you back, the night clerk looked upset?"

"Yes. Maybe he'd had time to think it over, and had begun to wonder. Or maybe by the time I got back there was something—not normal in the way I looked or acted. Anyway, he got that funny look on his face. Those two must have seen it."

And because they had seen it, I realized now, they had been eager to get away from the hotel. That was why they had not come into my room with me, and put me to bed, and hung the sweater and madras pants back in the wardrobe. If they had done that, if there had not been that heap of clothing beside my bed this morning, then I would have gone on believing that they had been no more than figures in an especially detailed and vivid dream.

That no doubt was what they had counted upon my believing. And so, after they left the hotel, they must have continued to worry about the night clerk. Would he, later on, question me about that visit from my "sister" and her companion?

I said to Eric, "They must have been afraid that the night clerk would talk to me about them."

He nodded. "And so they decided not to take any chances with the poor old guy."

For a moment we sat there silently, our untouched coffees cooling on the table between us. I turned and looked at the Place des Vosges. Three centuries ago Henri the Fourth's young courtiers, as if seized by some mass suicidal-murderous frenzy, used to fight dozens of simultaneous duels-to-the-death along those paths. Now young mothers and nursemaids wheeled baby carriages over the gravel, and old men frowned over chessboards set out on the benches, and a few men and women, neither old nor young, sat reading newspapers, or just soaking up the spring sunlight.

Eric said, "That girl. We know now why Gastand tried to kidnap you off the sidewalk yesterday morning, and why he took you to that place, wherever it was, last night."

I turned back to him. "Yes. It's because I look a lot like her. That's why they picked me." My throat closed up. After a moment I went on, "While I was coming down the subway steps this morning, I got the idea that they intended . . ." I broke off.

"I know," Eric said quietly. "They must intend that she'll be aboard that plane tomorrow, not you."

"No, Eric! If they planned that, I wouldn't be here now. They'd have kept me last night. They'd have—"

"Killed you? Honey, I don't want to scare you more than you are now. But I think that's exactly what Gastand intended when he tried to force you into that car. I don't think it was part of the other guy's plan, the one who seems to be the boss, from what you tell me. I think Gastand was acting on his own."

I thought of the quarreling voices of the two men,

fading in and out. "I think you're right." After a moment I asked, "Eric, what are we going to do?"

"Go to the American consul, of course, and dump the whole thing in his lap."

He placed coins beside his saucer. Then, as if sensing that I would not relish another subway ride just then, he stepped to the curb and, after a moment, flagged down a taxi.

Chapter 9

We were kept waiting in an outer office at the consulate for almost twenty minutes. I did not mind too much. True, as we traveled up sun-flooded Rue de Rivoli, I had kept wondering tensely if Eric, too, realized that someone might be following us through traffic, perhaps in a dark green Ford, perhaps in some other make of car. But when we stepped from the taxi before the impressive bulk of the American Embassy on Avenue Gabriel, the sight of American Marines guarding the portals had been reassuring. So, too, was the photograph of the President—ours, not France's—smiling benignly down from the walls of this office. Across the room an attractive brunette of thirty-five or so sat behind a desk. The clatter of her typewriter keys was the only sound, except the muted hum of traffic from beyond the long windows.

At last the brunette rose with a sheaf of papers in her hand and opened the door of an inner office. A few minutes later she reappeared, still with the papers, and sat down at her desk. "Mr. Creighton will see you now."

The inner office was small but elegant, with deep gold velours draperies, framed prints of Washington, D.C., in the nineteenth century on the walls, and a highly polished mahogany desk bare of everything except a telephone, a gold-and-onyx pen and pencil set, and the framed photograph of a blond, smiling young woman and a blond, glum-looking little boy. The slender, brown-haired young man who rose from his chair behind the desk was also elegant, in a dark suit that probably had been tailored on Saville Row. He wore a small white rose in his buttonhole.

"I'm George Creighton, the consul's assistant."

We gave our names. He shook hands with us and then waved us to chairs facing his desk. "Now what can I do for you?"

I took a deep breath. "I'm a stewardess for Columbia Airlines." Nervousness made my voice thin, mechanical. With dismay I realized that I sounded like a schoolgirl reciting something she had memorized. "After I left the airlines bus terminal yesterday morning, I started walking toward this bookstore about half a mile away. A dark green Ford with four men in it stopped at the curb . . ."

As I went on, I saw shock in his face, and then a growing doubt. Because there was nothing else to do, I plowed doggedly on. "And then Eric came up behind me—"

"I knocked the guy flat," Eric said. "The car drove away. Then two cops took us all to the police station."

As Eric described those tumultuous few minutes in

the station, I saw the doubt in Mr. Creighton's face harden into cold conviction. Eric must have seen it too, for his voice grew louder, as if he hoped to overwhelm the assistant consul's distrust with sheer decibels. He described leaving Wolfgang at the pet shop, and then our dash down the Metro steps and our circuitous underground journey to Boulevard St.-Germain. "We went into a café and talked, and after a while Dorothy decided to spend the night at this little hotel near there." He turned to me. "Tell him what happened last night."

I told him. By now his face had become an expressionless mask. I knew that the color I felt in my own face must reinforced his conviction that either we were mad or that we had come here to make a fool of him and insult the dignity of the consulate with an elaborate practical joke.

At last he said, "That police station. Is it in the Eighth Arrondissement?"

Eric said, "That's right."

Wordlessly Mr. Creighton got up and walked into the outer office, closing the door behind him. In mute distress, I looked at Eric. He gave me a forced-looking smile. "It'll be all right. Sooner or later he'll believe us."

Mr. Creighton was gone for a long time, perhaps ten minutes. When he came back in, he sat down behind his desk and then said, "Well, the commissaire there confirms your account of what happened at the police station. Now if—notice that I say *if*—you made up the rest of it because you're afraid of

100

being sent to jail for your behavior, knocking down a respectable businessman on the street—"

Eric made a sound deep in his throat. Fortunately, it was unintelligible.

"—and allowing your dog to attack a police official—" He broke off, apparently lost in a forest of syntax. "What I am saying," he resumed, "is that if you're afraid of arrest, you can relax. The police have agreed not to pursue the matter. That is, if you cause no more trouble."

Eric had gotten his temper under control. "I didn't make up anything, Mr. Creighton, and I'm sure Dorothy didn't either."

"No, I didn't. Maybe I'm crazy." My voice shook. "Several times since yesterday morning I've thought I might be. But I'm not lying. I've told you what I think happened."

His expression softened somewhat. "Very well, Miss Wanger. But what I can't understand is this. If you think that not only you but your airline may be the target of some sort of—machination, why haven't you laid this whole matter before them? If they gave credence to your story, then certainly we would, and we would give the airline and the police all the necessary cooperation. But instead you come to me, admittedly with no witness to back you up, and tell me a story of having been driven somewhere, you don't know where, to some house or apartment, you don't even know which . . ." He broke off. Plainly, he was becoming angry all over again.

I said, "I did try to contact the airline! There's this very good friend of mine, Jim Henderson. He's a Columbia pilot, and his brother-in-law is on the board of directors. He's registered at the International. I tried to call him several times yesterday and last night, and again this morning, but he's out somewhere."

He picked up the phone. "The International, you say? Do you know the number?"

I gave it to him. He dialed, waited a moment, and then said in French, "May I please speak to Mr. James Henderson?" Then, after a few more seconds, he handed the phone to me with a frosty little smile.

Damn Jim! He had stayed out all night, and then returned just in time to make me look even more like a liar in the eyes of that elegant man behind the desk. I said into the phone, "Jim, it's Dorothy."

"Dottikins! Where have you been? I just saw Mimi in the lobby, and she and I were wondering what particular haystack—"

"Jim, Eric and I have got to see you."

"Eric? Is that on again? Mimi said it might be." Even though he spoke lightly, I could tell he didn't like the idea.

"No, it isn't. Listen to me, Jim. This is very serious. We've got to see you right away."

After a moment he said, "How about the bar here at the International? Can you make it in half an hour?"

"Yes. Thank you, Jim." I hung up.

Plainly eager to be rid of us, Mr. Creighton got to

his feet. "Good-bye, Miss Wanger, Mr. Lang." He did not offer to shake hands. "As I told you, if the airline wishes our cooperation in this matter, they will of course have it." His slight smile made it clear that he did not expect to hear from the airline.

Chapter 10

LESS than half an hour later we climbed red-carpeted stairs leading up from Rue de Castiglione to the Belle-Époque splendor of the International's lobby. We turned left, moved along a glass wall shielding a large courtyard with tables set around a fountain, and then to our right toward the bar.

A few people sat in the big, softly lighted room enjoying a pre-luncheon apéritif. One of the hostesses, a young woman with straight brown hair falling below her shoulders, approached us. She was beautiful enough to have occupied one of those flower-bedecked giant bird cages they lower from the ceiling at the Folies Bergère. She led us to a leather-upholstered banquette against one wall. Before she could take our order, Jim Henderson walked up to the table, broad-shouldered in a green-and-navy checked sports jacket and dark slacks. Little as he deserved it, he had the healthy, wholesome look of an advance man for a Billy Graham rally.

"Hello, you two." Then to the hostess: "Hiya, gorgeous." I knew from that that she was not one of his conquests. If she had been, he would have called her "dear."

We gave our order, Scotch and water for the men and coffee for me. When a white-jacketed bus boy had placed the glasses and my coffee cup before us, Jim said, "Now what's this all about?"

I did most of the talking, with Eric interrupting now and then to add a detail. Jim listened, his thinning brown hair glossy under the dim amber light, his broad face stunned.

When I stopped speaking, Jim said with a smile, "Be sure to tell me what sort of pills you two have been popping. I want to steer clear of them." But I saw that his eyes were not smiling. They were sober —and worried.

I said, "Don't hand us that, Jim. I can tell you don't think it was a pipe dream."

"You're right. Twelve years or so ago I wouldn't have believed you. But back then I wouldn't have believed there would be all these assassinations, or that three Presidents in a row, one way or another, would get knocked out of the box before their innings were over, or that some beautiful rich doll would join up with some revolutionary weirdos to rob a bank, or that a bunch of Arabs in bed sheets would be buying up Wall Street, practically." He shook his head. "It's a screwy world, and getting screwier."

"That's a sound bit of social commentary," Eric said. "Unoriginal, but sound."

I shot him an apprehensive look. Even before my divorce from Eric, I had been aware that he and Jim disliked each other. Since the divorce, Jim had adopted a moralistic attitude, which on him looked about as fitting as a bishop's miter on Hugh Hefner, toward Eric's betrayal of his marriage vows. The result was a frequent exchange of barbed remarks which, if they had been women, would have been considered catty.

"But to get back to the matter in hand," Eric went on. "What do you think is behind it? Drugs?"

Jim's lip curled slightly. "Do you mean, are they planning that some ringer for Dottie will smuggle drugs into Kennedy? No way. Neither drugs, nor diamonds, nor anything else. Because airline personnel have the best chance to smuggle, customs goes over their luggage with a fine-toothed comb. Dottie can confirm that."

I nodded.

"What then?" Eric asked. "Something political?"

"Another assassination attempt, you mean? Could be. Anything could be. But it seems damned unlikely that anyone would send a girl to do the job."

"A hijack?"

"There are far simpler ways for a hijacker to get aboard. Besides, surely no one would pick a girl to hijack a 747."

I said, "What—what shall we do about it?"

"Why, make damned sure that no ringer boards that plane tomorrow. And in order to make sure ... But first, I want to check on something. What was the name of that old hotel clerk?"

"Dubois, I think. Armand Dubois."

"Excuse me while I make a phone call."

When Jim had gone, I said, "Don't start needling him. This is no time for that."

"I know. But just the sight of that guy raises my blood pressure."

To change the subject I asked, "When are you going to get Wolfgang out of that pet shop?"

"When I get back from New York."

"New York!"

"I'm going to be on that plane tomorrow too. Once I'm in New York, I'll call the Cartmill people and explain. I wasn't supposed to report to their office here for another week, anyhow."

"All that expense," I said, but my protest was a feeble one. This was one time I would be glad to have Eric aboard my flight. A so-and-so he might be, and, what was more, a so-and-so with two left feet, but I'd been glad of his protection on that sidewalk yesterday morning, and might find myself glad of it again.

"To hell with the expense," Eric said.

We sat in silence until Jim returned. He slid onto the curved leather seat, not smiling now. "I phoned the police. He's dead, all right. Hit-and-run. The taxi driver who saw it says that it was a sedan. The light wasn't strong enough for him to be sure of the make, or whether it was black or some other dark color."

He paused, and then went on, "I also phoned the Champs Élysées office." Columbia's Paris headquarters were on the Champs Élysées. "They said for all three of us to hustle right over there. And after that, Dottikins, we're going to keep you on ice until you're aboard that plane tomorrow afternoon."

"On ice?" I tried to smile. "But I'm in no danger. If they intended to—harm me, they'd have done it last night."

I saw the two men exchange uncomfortable looks. Then Eric covered his hand with mine and said, "It's like this, honey. If that bald guy is running things, he must have figured that last night was—too soon. What if I'd called the hotel today and found you missing? I'd have notified the police, and the American consul, and the airline. With a flock of people out at Roissy waiting to question you about where you had been, they'd have had almost no chance to get a ringer aboard in your place tomorrow."

"If that's what they plan," Jim said. "Personally, I don't see how they could hope to pull it off."

"Sure," Eric said, with that edge in his voice, "if that's what they plan."

The full import of what Eric had said sunk in. As far as the bald man was concerned, last night had been "too soon." They planned to let me stay free—and alive—until almost plane time. And then—

My hand turned palm upward and fastened around Eric's hand. I said, "Then someone must be —keeping track of me. Someone must have followed me from the hotel to the Place des Vosges, and then followed you and me to the consulate, and then—"

I looked around the big, softly lighted room. That man up there at the bar, talking with the beautiful hostess? Those two men in a banquette almost directly opposite us, with what looked like business papers spread out on the table?

Jim said, "Stop looking around like that. No one's going to harm you before witnesses. They'd never in the world get a fake Dorothy Wanger aboard then. You'll be in danger only if you're alone, the way you were on the street yesterday, and at that hotel last night. And from now on you're not going to be alone. You'll stay here in a room with a private cop outside your door until it's time for you to drive out to Roissy under heavy escort."

"It's okay about the cop," Eric said. "But he'll stay at my place. Dorothy's staying with me, not just until she gets to Roissy, but until she gets to New York."

After a moment Jim said, smiling, "For an ex-husband, you're a little shirty, aren't you? I think it's up to Dottie where she stays."

Perhaps it was because I was tired, and frightened, and confused. Perhaps it was because I felt that even a bodyguard would not be adequate protection in this huge place, with its scores of employees, its hundreds of people moving through the lobby and along the corridors. Anyway, I heard myself say, "I'll stay at Eric's place tonight."

Chapter 11

LATE that afternoon Eric and I and a man named Carl Bettzinger approached a beautiful old wrought-iron gate a stone's throw from notorious Rue Pigalle. The gate was unlatched. As Eric opened it, the faintly mustached concierge in her little booth just beyond the gate said good day to him, cast a mildly curious glance at Carl Bettzinger and me, and then returned her attention to the pink thread and flashing crochet needle in her hands.

To go through the gate was like returning to the earliest years of the century, when Montmartre was famous, not for its striptease joints and streetwalkers, but for the artists and writers and musicians who lived on these heights overlooking Paris. On either side of the broad path, well-kept stone or stucco houses of varying architectural styles stood behind their small lawns. Evidently practitioners of the arts still lived here, because as we moved up the path, with Bettzinger a step or two in the rear, I saw, affixed to a cement gatepost, a brass plate announcing that the premises were occupied by the Bourget

110

School of the Drama. Next door, from beyond a balconied second-floor window, an unseen pianist played several bars of a Beethoven sonata, paused, and repeated the passage.

Carl Bettzinger was the private cop who had been assigned to us—more specifically to me—at the meeting in Columbia's Champs Élysées offices that afternoon. For me that meeting had been a strange but comforting experience. Only that morning, there on the subway platform, I had been alone with my nightmarish fear of everyone around me. Now I sat in a large, sunny room, filled with airline officials and with representatives of the Paris metropolitan police and the French Sûreté. The American consul had sent a representative too—not Mr. Creighton, but an older and less dapper man named Forbes.

None of these men gave my story full credence. I could read doubt in every face. But plainly they shared Jim Henderson's attitude. In today's turbulent world, they simply dared not assume that I was psychotic, or that Eric and I were perpetrators of a hoax. And so they had me repeat several times every detail I could recall about Gastand's and the girl's invasion of my hotel room, and that ride through the nighttime streets, and that almost-gaudy room where I had stood docilely beside the girl, my eyes dazzled by the flash of the camera in the bald man's hands. Several of them tried to jog my recollection about what sort of car Gastand had driven, and the location of the private house or apartment to which he had taken me. It was no use. What I sensed were long stretches of the night remained blank in my memory.

At last Eric and I were allowed to go, accompanied by the man who would be responsible for my safety for the next twenty-four hours. I knew that the men we had left would now get down to the details of how they would handle any eventuality at either Roissy or Kennedy.

In the ticket office on the ground floor, Bettzinger and I stood beside Eric while he bought his ticket for the next day's three o'clock flight. Thanks to a party of more than a hundred globe-trotting Japanese, the last seat in economy class had been sold two hours earlier. With an inward shudder, I watched Eric sign traveler's checks for a first-class ticket.

Over a belated lunch in a café next door to the airline offices, we learned a little about Bettzinger. A burly, shy-mannered bachelor in his mid-forties, he looked like a truck driver on vacation. Instead, he had been a member of the New York police force for nearly a decade. Then, twelve years ago, he had come to Paris for a week, fallen in love with the city, and never returned to New York. He had worked as a security man for the Paris branches of several American companies. For the past three years he had been employed by Columbia.

Toward the end of the meal he shed some of his shyness and began to ask businesslike questions about Eric's apartment. It was a duplex, Eric told him, with a living room, kitchen, and dining nook on the first floor, and two bedrooms and a bath on the

112

second. Yes, there was a rear door leading to a small, high-fenced service area. The one-floor apartment above the duplex was occupied by two women— retired English schoolteachers.

Now we went up a narrow brick path to a house of tan stucco. On the little brick porch, Eric unlocked the door. I walked past him into a large room, pleasantly furnished with end tables and a coffee table in walnut, and a sofa and armchairs slipcovered in faded chintz. Eric's tenancy had been too brief for him to leave much of his mark upon the room. Only books taken down from the wall shelves and left on the coffee table and the sofa, and a copy of *Paris Soir* standing tentlike on the floor, testified to his ability to reduce any room to chaos.

Carl laid his hat, a brown felt, on an end table. "You two better wait here," he said. Moving with a swiftness surprising in a man so burly, he went into what I assumed was the kitchen. I heard him opening a door, and then, after a few moments, closing it and turning a key in a lock. He came back into the living room and climbed the stairs.

When he returned to us a few minutes later, he said, "All clear. Keep your bedroom windows locked tonight." He looked at the sofa. "I'd better sleep down here on the first floor."

Eric took my suitcase up to one of the bedrooms. It looked austere, with its monk's cloth bedspread and its circa 1910 golden oak bureau, but comfortable enough. When Eric had left me, I took my uniform from my suitcase and hung it in the closet so

113

that it would be wrinkle-free by the next afternoon. After a shower in the small tiled bathroom down the hall, I returned to my room and dressed, putting on the brown skirt, but substituting a cotton shirt of lighter brown for the jersey turtleneck.

I had just descended the stairs when the phone rang. Eric lifted it from its cradle and then beckoned to me to stand close, so that I could hear both sides of the conversation.

"—all squared away," Jim Henderson was saying. "Roissy will be crawling with extra guards tomorrow. They're shifting two of those Japanese to first class so that extra security men will ride in economy. And they're beefing up security at Kennedy, too."

"Any specific reason for more security at Kennedy?"

"Yes. The thinking seems to be that they might fly the blonde over by another plane, wait until after Dottie has cleared customs, and *then* try to pull a switch. But they won't have a prayer at either the Paris or the New York end. Probably they realize that. If one of them has kept an eye on Dottie today, and I'm sure someone has, then they know there was some sort of powwow between airline officials and the police at Columbia's offices today. Whatever they were up to, it's almost certain that they've canceled it. I suppose that's why Gastand flew the coop."

"Gastand? Haven't the police picked him up?"

"No. This woman assistant at his shop said that he flew to Madrid this morning to look at some seventeenth-century furniture."

114

"Is the woman assistant—"

"She's not the blonde. She's fiftyish, and a Roumanian refugee. She says that he goes on a buying trip to Spain and Portugal every year about this time, and the charge account he has with Iberian Airlines bears her out. He has no police record. I gather that so far there's no evidence except Dottie's to indicate that he's anything but what he says he is —an antique dealer."

Again that sickening self-doubt brushed me. If, prompted only by hallucination, I had set all these forces in motion . . .

A moment later I felt better, because I heard Jim say, "They may have something on the bald guy with the tic, though. Dottie's description checks with that of a certain Emile Lavery, present whereabouts unknown. Although he's not a big-time crook—I guess you could call him middle-time—he has a record a yard long."

Eric asked, "For what?"

"Diamond smuggling, drugs, gun running, you name it. About five years ago, in New York, he got himself in trouble with the police, and even worse trouble with the local Mafia. If he hadn't been deported, he'd have wound up in a New Jersey meadow. At least that's the information the New York police got from their informers."

I thought of the quarreling voices of the two men, fading in and out there in the room with the smoked mirrors. "I can't go to New York," the bald man had said. If he were Emile Lavery, then the reason was clear. In New York he would have deadlier enemies than the police to worry about.

"How's Dottie?"

Eric's tone became curt. "She's fine."

"Listen, Lang. You had your innings there, and you struck out. Why don't you let her alone for a while and give some other guy a chance?"

"Like who, for instance? Some divorced, forty-year-old makeout artist?"

"Look who's calling who divorced. And I'm not forty yet. Besides, a guy can change, can't he?"

"I wouldn't bet on it."

Jim's laugh held a nasty edge. "One thing's for sure, old buddy boy. I'd never pull what you did. Cheating is one thing that shouldn't be kept all in the family. No, Dottie didn't tell me. I guessed."

Eric's voice was thick. "What do you mean, you guessed?"

"I was at your wedding, remember? So was Natalie Wanger. Maybe you didn't realize it, but you two gave each other one of those unfinished-business looks. Right there in the line at the church door, buddy boy, with your little bride standing beside you."

"You're a damned liar! I don't even remember Natalie in that line. I know she must have been there, but I don't remember her."

"Hell, let it go. Put Bettzinger on, will you? I'd better brief him too."

Eric laid down the phone and turned to me. "Dottie, I swear—"

116

"What does it matter now?" And yet it did. It hurt me to think that Eric and Natalie, even on my wedding day, had felt a stir of interest in each other. "I'd better see what food there is," I said, and turned toward the kitchen.

Dinner that night, assembled by me from canned and frozen food Eric had bought the day before, consisted of broiled fish, green peas, and peach halves in a too-sweet syrup. The meal was as uncomfortable as it was undistinguished. For one thing, Bettzinger resisted all suggestions that he divest himself of his winterweight sports jacket. Perhaps he feared that the sight of his shoulder holster, its bulk visible through the brown-and-green striped cloth, might offend. For another thing, he volunteered no remarks whatever, but only answered, in painful monosyllables, the questions asked him.

After dinner, both men offered to dry dishes. Fearing for Jake Sommers' china, I chose Bettzinger. Still wearing his jacket, he moved about the small kitchen with that surprising deftness, stacking plates almost noiselessly, and spreading the dish towel to dry when we had finished.

We returned to the living room, where Eric informed us that the audio was out on the TV set. At my rather desperate suggestion, we searched the drawers of the desk in one corner until we found a deck of cards, repaired to the dining nook, and began to play poker, with matches representing one-tenth-of-a-cent each as our chips. However lacking in conversation, Carl was no slouch at cards. By ten o'clock he had all the matches, and Eric and I were each eighty cents poorer.

When I suggested to Carl that it was time for me to make up his bed on the sofa, he said hastily that he could do that himself. I believed him. He struck me as one of those bachelors who could make their own soap if they chose to. "All right." I turned to Eric. "I'll get out sheets and blankets, if you'll show me where they are."

Eric and I went upstairs to the linen closet in the hall. While I was piling sheets, a pillowcase, and light blankets onto his extended forearms, he said, "Dottie."

I knew that tone. "Please don't, Eric."

"It's just that I haven't been able to stop loving you. And you still love me. If you didn't, you wouldn't have come here. You'd be at the International now. I don't know why you still feel that way, but you do."

I didn't know why, either. He broke things. He was intelligent, but not brilliant. He'd never be rich. He wasn't particularly handsome. He'd shared a bed with my own sister. And yet—there it was.

I felt the pressure of tears behind my eyes. "I wish I had stayed at the International."

"Honey—"

He reached out for me. I said, drawing back, "Watch it! You're going to drop the blankets."

He took a firmer hold on his burden. "Just listen, then. We belong together. We were happy once. You can't deny that, can you?"

I remained silent. No, I couldn't deny that.

118

"We could be that happy again." When I still didn't answer, he said bitterly, "It's that bastard Jim Henderson. If he hadn't said what he did over the phone today—"

"Don't blame Jim. I didn't need him to tell me that from the first I was second-best with you. For nearly a year now I've realized that if you thought Natalie was interested in you that night we met, you would never even have looked at me."

He said after a moment, "Maybe not. But that was then. Later on I—"

"And that time at Bridgehampton. If Natalie had told you she loved you, would you have wanted to stay with me?"

"Of course I would have!"

"Are you absolutely sure, Eric? Oh, you might have agonized over the choice for weeks, even months. But are you sure that in the end you wouldn't have chosen her?"

"For God's sake, Dottie!"

"Well?"

His eyes were wretched behind their hornrims. "You're asking the impossible. Of course I can't be absolutely sure. How could anyone be sure of what he might have done in the case of something that never happened?"

The pressure of tears was an ache now. "Please, Eric. Maybe it's partly because she was my own sister. But anyway, I could never get over this feeling of—of being second-best. So please don't hound me any more. Please don't."

He said heavily after a long moment, "All right. Once you're safely in New York, I'll leave you alone. If we ever run into each other, here in Paris or anywhere else, you'll know it was an accident."

He stood there for a moment more, as if waiting for me to speak. Then, with the blankets in his arms, he turned and went down the stairs. I crossed the hall to my room.

Long after I went to bed, I lay awake. The night was very quiet. Only the occasional muted sound of a taxi horn or police siren came through the closed window to remind that a few hundred yards away, lights and music spilled from open doorways, and taxi-loads of tourists streamed into cabarets in search of Montmartre's wicked delights.

Somehow I was sure that Eric would keep his promise. It was what I wanted. The world was full of men. After six months or so of not seeing him, surely I would be able to think of him almost with indifference.

It was only now, filled with awareness of him in that other bedroom down the hall, that I felt lonely and desolate.

I turned over in bed and finally drifted off to sleep.

Chapter 12

I AWOKE to gray light and to rain so heavy that it ran down the window in an unbroken sheet. My watch said eight-fifteen. In less than seven hours, I would be in a plane soaring over the tidy French countryside toward the Atlantic.

And for the last time. Somewhere on the unconscious level I must have come to that decision, because as I lay there, gaze fixed on the wavering, translucent sheet of water on the other side of the windowpane, I found that my mind was made up. From now on, Eric and I would not see each other, even accidentally. If Columbia would not transfer me to the New York–London flight or some other run, then I would quit.

Someone knocked very softly. "Are you awake?"

"Yes." I sat up in bed.

He had trouble getting the door open. A moment later I saw why. He carried a breakfast tray of dark wood. On it was a small glass of orange juice, an egg in its china cup, two pieces of toast, blackened at the edges, a coffee cup and saucer, silver, and a jelly glass holding two pink petunias. Their petals, frayed at the edges, bore white spots.

As he set the tray across my knees, my throat tightened. How unfair he was. I pictured him out there in the rain, gathering those ridiculous, beat-up petunias.

"The flowers aren't much," he apologized. "They were all I could find in the little garden out back. I meant the egg to be soft-boiled, the way you like it, but maybe, while I was out looking for flowers . . ."

With my knife I struck off the top of the egg. Its solid center stared up at me like a pale yellow eye. My throat grew even tighter.

Women were fools. At least I was. Why should his very ineptitude make me want to cry?

"Hey, don't look like that. I'll fix you another egg."

"This one's fine." I took a sip of orange juice and then dug my spoon into crumbling egg yolk.

"The airline phoned. They'll check by phone again at one o'clock, and they'll send a car for you at two. You won't go aboard until the last moment, after they've made sure there's no one on that plane who shouldn't be."

He paused. "Is your VW parked at Kennedy?"

"Yes."

"Well, since I'll be in first class, I'll probably get off the plane and through customs before you. Will you meet me in the terminal coffee shop and let me ride with you to your apartment? I swear I'll leave you as soon as you're inside your door. I just want to make sure you get home safe."

He waited there with that earnest, wretched look on his face. I thought, I've got to get out of here. Otherwise, sometime during the next almost seven hours, I might find myself doing something irretrievably stupid, like crying in his arms.

"All right." Then: "Do we have to stay here this morning? Can't we go out somewhere?"

He looked at the streaming window. "Out? Where?"

I said, unable to think of anything else, "The *Bateaux-mouches.*"

"You want to go down the river in a sightseeing boat? In the rain?"

"Why not? Those boats are glassed-in. And I haven't been down the river in a long time." That was not true. Only two weeks before, Jim Henderson and I, together with Mimi and a young New York lawyer who had been a recent passenger on our flight, had taken the dinner trip down the Seine. We had dined at a flower-decked table, while the quays of Paris with their floodlighted palaces and other public buildings had slid past. Perhaps because I had not seen Eric for several months previous to that evening, I had been able to enjoy it thoroughly.

"Well, okay, if that's what you want. We'll have to check with Carl, though. And he'll have to go with us. His orders are to stick close until you're aboard that plane."

"I don't think he'll object to the idea of a boat trip. You know what Jim said. Everyone thinks there's no longer any danger."

123

"Well, Carl's having breakfast. I'll go ask him."

He left me. With my knife, I began to scrape the blackened edges of a piece of toast into my saucer.

When I carried the tray down to the kitchen, I learned that Carl had agreed, although somewhat reluctantly, to the boat trip. I went back to my room and took from the bottom of my suitcase the garments I had found indispensable in Paris—a transparent, hooded raincoat and knee-high black rain boots.

Twenty minutes later a taxi carried us down Rue Pigalle. In his dark blue raincoat, Eric sat beside me. His Leica camera in its brown leather case hung from a strap around his neck. Bettzinger rode up front, his burly shoulders straining the seams of an ancient black slicker and his felt hat protected by one of those transparent plastic covers. Eric had unearthed both articles, doubtless the property of his friend Jake Sommers, from a closet under the stairs.

Wicked Rue Pigalle looked melancholy under the rain. No magnificently arrayed doormen stood at the cabarets' closed portals, and the sidewalks were almost deserted. The taxi turned onto Avenue Royale for a stretch, and then drove to the boat dock near the Alma Bridge. A boat was tied up at the landing. Through the glass-enclosed side of the lower deck we could see that even on this inclement day, a few people were aboard. When Eric had bought our tickets at a wooden booth on the dock, we went up the gangway.

The lower deck smelled of raincoats and of hot

chocolate from the vending machine. Most of the long benches stretched emptily away in the center aisle. The loud-speaker uttered a few preliminary squawks. Soon, as we glided down the river, the loud-speaker would give us, in French and English, an account of palaces and churches and bridges representing a thousand years of history.

Deckhands on the wharf let go the lines. While Eric and I stood at the railing in the space beyond the front rows of seats, with Bettzinger standing a few feet away, the boat began to glide through the rain at a sedate half-dozen miles an hour. I saw the Eiffel Tower melt into the gray curtain, and then the Chamber of Deputies' gold dome take shape. The few other passengers sat thirty feet away, near the stairs leading to the top deck. I could not hear their conversation. The only sound was the metallic voice on the loud-speaker, the engine's throb, and the faint swish of water past the hull.

I did not talk to Eric, or he to me. But I was acutely aware of him standing there in his dark blue raincoat. It was the same one he had left in a restaurant, and had to go back for, the night we met. It was strange how rain seemed a part of every turning point in my relationship with Eric. Glistening reflection of neon on rain-wet Madison Avenue that first night I went out with him. A gray drizzle falling that morning when I sat huddled on the damp sand at Bridge-hampton. And rain falling on this, the last day we would see each other.

The boat glided between the Left Bank and the

Cathedral of Notre-Dame on its river island. Today in the rain, that great gray mass, built by thousands of wholehearted believers in the Age of Faith, had a melancholy look. It reminded me of some noble prehistoric beast, meant to live in the primeval forest, which had somehow survived into the era of smog and traffic jams.

The rain began to slacken as we passed the tip of the island and glided on beneath a series of vaulted bridges. It had stopped almost entirely by the time the time the boat turned and started back toward the Alma Bridge.

Perhaps to enjoy a different vantage point on the return trip, a couple moved from the far end of the boat's cabin and sat down on a bench a few feet from Eric and me. The girl, who wore a shiny new wedding ring, could not have been more than eighteen. Her husband was perhaps two or three years older. Provincial newlyweds, obviously, on their wedding trip. They were both plain, and they wore their new, cheap-looking clothing awkwardly. And yet as they sat there, hands clasped, it was obvious from the bliss on their faces that each regarded the other as the most desirable person in the world.

I felt a dull ache in my heart, and identified it as envy. Perhaps it would have been best, after all, if we had stayed at Eric's flat.

I said, "The rain's stopped. Let's go up on deck."

The three of us climbed the stairs. Now watery sunlight gleamed on the wet deck with its rows of empty benches, and on the gray-blue water and the windows of buildings lining the Right Bank. Eric and I at the rail, with Carl standing a few feet from us, watched the river traffic. A barge going in the opposite direction, with a woman—some optimist who believed there would be no more rain that day—hanging shirts on a line strung above the foredeck. A speedboat, its engine throttled so that it kept pace with us. Another barge moving downstream, its deck loaded with iron pipes.

Eric said, "Mind if I ask Carl to take our picture?"

So that was why he had brought his camera along on this rainy day. One final snapshot to file away with those taken in Bermuda, and in the New York apartment, and on the beach at Bridgehampton. I said, "All right."

Carl took the camera willingly. "Suppose I stand on the end of a bench," he said, "and get a shot of you two looking up."

He turned and looked forward, apparently to make sure that the central arch of the bridge ahead was high enough to accommodate a man standing eighteen inches or so above deck level. Then he climbed up on a bench and aimed the camera at us.

"Stand back a little farther, so I can get your feet in."

Obediently we stepped back. From somewhere to the left, out on the river, I heard the roar of a suddenly accelerating engine.

"Okay," Carl said, "give me a big smile."

Stretching my lips, I gazed up at the camera.

The boat swerved. Only a little, but enough.

"Watch out!" I screamed.

It was too late. The curving edge of the ancient stone arch struck the back of Carl's head. With the camera flying from his hand, he fell from his perch to lie sprawled in the aisle between the rows of benches.

Chapter 13

Eric and I knelt on either side of him. The impact had knocked his hat with its transparent cover from his head, revealing a small bald spot, which I had not noticed before, in the curly brown hair. Between the two of us, had we killed him, this shy, serious man? At my insistence, we had gone on this wretched boat trip. And then Eric, with his damned camera . . . Fleetingly I was aware of it, lying over there under a bench. It was in two pieces now.

Carl moaned and stirred slightly.

A white-faced deckhand was beside us now. He said, in French, "Better turn him over and move him onto a bench."

With Eric supporting his shoulders and the deckhand his feet, they carried him to a bench near where the pilot sat at the wheel, and stretched him out. His eyes were open now, staring up at us with a puzzled expression.

"It's a good thing we were going so slow," the deckhand said, "and a good thing he was wearing a hat. There's a doctor's office not far from the Alma Bridge. You'd better get him there as soon as you can." He paused, and then asked, "Did you see that speedboat?"

Eric asked, "What speedboat?"

"One with two fellows in it. It swerved toward us and then shot through the bridge's side arch. Probably they're two miles downriver by now. We get jokers like that. Just because they can rent a boat for fifty francs an hour, they think they own the river."

I felt a cold ripple down my backbone. Jokers? Or two men who weren't joking at all? Two men who, sometimes ahead of us, sometimes behind, sometimes alongside, had kept close to the sightseeing boat ever since it had left the dock. Men who had seen our guardian up there on the bench, and had decided to make the pilot swerve a little off course . . .

"We get that kind on American lakes and rivers too," Eric said. If his thoughts had paralleled mine, neither his face nor voice gave any sign of it.

By the time the boat reached the landing, Carl was sitting up, still with that dazed look on his face. With me following, Eric and the deckhand helped him off the boat and up the gentle incline to the quay. I waved frantically at the first cab in line at a taxi station about a hundred feet to my left. The cab moved forward and stopped beside us.

When Eric and I were in the back seat, with our still-silent bodyguard between us, the deckhand gave the driver an address on Avenue Montaigne.

As the cab pulled away from the curb, Carl said, "Where—"

"We're taking you to a doctor," Eric told him.

"No! I've got to get you two back to your flat."

"Plenty of time for that. Just take it easy."

A moment later Carl said, looking at the now-empty leather case which dangled from Eric's neck, "I must have busted your camera, huh?"

"Forget it. It was insured."

The cab stopped beside one of a row of houses with mansard roofs. When Eric and I had guided Carl across the broad, tree-shadowed sidewalk, we saw a brass plate beside the door. It announced that Dr. Bertrand occupied apartment five. In the impressively broad ground-floor hall, obeying the injunction of the card affixed to the door of number five, I pressed the bell and opened the door.

A white-capped nurse seated at a desk on the far side of the pleasant waiting room, with its sofas and armchairs slipcovered in beige linen, got to her feet at sight of us. "It's an emergency," Eric said. "A head injury."

She crossed the room and took my place beside Carl. They helped him inside the inner office. Almost immediately Eric reappeared, his face as guilty and worried as I knew mine must be. For perhaps twenty minutes we sat there on one of the sofas, aware that the room's two other occupants, well-dressed women of middle age, raised their eyes from their magazines every now and then to throw us a curious glance. Then a white-coated man, blond and youngish,

131

opened the door of the inner office and beckoned to us.

We found Carl, less pale now, strectched out on a black leather couch. "He'll be all right," the doctor said. "However, I would advise his checking with his own doctor tomorrow. And he should remain lying down for the next half hour."

"No!" Carl sat up and swung his feet to the floor. When the doctor put a restraining hand on his shoulder, he looked up at Eric and said, "The airline's going to phone at one o'clock. If I'm not there, there'll be hell to pay."

I thought, feeling guiltier than ever, he's afraid of losing his job. Eric must have had the same thought, because he said, "Don't worry. We'll cover for you."

"No!" Carl shook off the doctor's hand and got to his feet. "It's past twelve now. I've got to—" He swayed, turned a greenish color, and sat down.

"You see?" Dr. Bertrand's voice was not without satisfaction. "Now lie down."

Carl obeyed. Eric grasped my arm. "We'll be there in plenty of time for the phone call," he said to our recumbent watchdog. "And if you get to the flat as soon as you feel up to it, they'll never know the difference."

It was not until we were out on Avenue Montaigne, and moving toward the intersection, that I said, "Eric, that speedboat—"

"I know what you thought. But you're wrong. They were the same sort of idiots you see endangering other boatmen on Long Island Sound."

132

"How can you be so—"

"Because even if someone had followed us to the dock, it wouldn't make sense to follow us on the river. All anyone would have had to do was to wait near the Alma Bridge dock until the sightseeing boat came back."

His words made sense. And yet, as we walked swiftly along the sidewalk, I was aware that he, too, was more tense than he had been an hour earlier, and that he kept scanning the traffic.

We had to walk at least two hundred yards before we found a taxi. The driver took us through the Place de la Concorde, now filled with lunchtime traffic. That paved open space, the scene of so many violent events in the past, was now jammed with angry drivers. Forbidden by law to sound their horns, they glared and shouted at each other as, at the direction of arm-waving police, they made their snail-like progress around the obelisk. Eric kept looking at his watch. Once he said, "We could have taken the Metro, if I'd known where the nearest station was."

"I didn't know either."

Once through the Place de la Concorde, we made fairly good time along Rue Royale and the maze of other streets leading north. But just as we were about to turn off Boulevard de Clichy into Place Pigalle, there was the grinding sound of metal against metal somewhere up ahead. Our line of traffic and the one next to it slowed, came to a halt.

Eric poked his head out of the window. When he withdrew it, he said, "Two cabs have locked bump-

133

ers. The drivers are out in the street arguing."

We looked at each other with sharpened anxiety. If the average French motorist is aggressive, and he is, French cabbies are downright warlike. Neither of those two would get in his taxi and drive off until a policeman appeared to straighten out the mess.

"We'll make better time walking," Eric said. He paid the driver, and we got out. With my raincoat over my arm, I crossed the little square with him and started up Rue Pigalle.

Now that the sun was out, the Montmartre district had come to life. Heavily made-up girls, in boots and outmoded mini skirts, with real or false hair brushing their shoulders, waited in doorways. Pedestrians, most of them lone males, eyed the girls, or turned into *"les sexy shoppes,"* with their discreetly drawn blinds behind their empty showcase windows, or lingered before displays of porno books and magazines. We had just passed a shop window offering almost unbelievable lingerie—all of it scarlet, with cutouts here and there—when Eric thrust me into a narrow doorway so abruptly that I staggered sideways against a steel mesh gate guarding the foot of a flight of dingy stairs. Back turned to the sidewalk, he placed a hand against each of the doorway's uprights, screening me from the view of anyone on the street.

I clung to the steel gate. "What—"

"A dark green Ford." His face was pale. "It just turned the corner into this street."

Chapter 14

Wᴇ stood there, not speaking, anxious eyes locked. Almost no danger, Jim Henderson and the others had said. But maybe they had miscalculated. Stomach tightened into a knot, I thought of bullets slamming into Eric's back and, as he pitched forward, other bullets finding me where I stood, fingers enmeshed in the steel gate. No, that could not happen. Not now, only a little more than two hours before flight time, and with only a few hundred yards separating us from the comparative safety of Eric's flat.

Cautiously he turned his head. "They've gone past. I can see the license plate. Seven-seven-something-zero. Now they're turning into Place Pigalle."

Relief made me so weak I had to tighten my grip on the gate. "Let's run to the flat."

"And maybe get caught out in the open? They'll probably circle back."

So they had followed us to the dock, and perhaps, despite what Eric had said, onto the river. Then somehow, between the Alma Bridge dock and the

135

doctor's office, our cab had lost them in traffic. Now they were cruising this neighborhood, hoping to find us before we could reach that enclave beyond the wrought-iron gate. Again I thought, with useless regret, of how I had insisted upon leaving the flat.

Eric had turned and was looking across the street. Beyond an open doorway, in full and inviting view of passers-by, a girl sat with her back turned to a small bar upholstered in dark leather, the sort you might find in an elaborately furnished apartment. Her face, extremely attractive and almost free of makeup, was framed in auburn hair that reached below her shoulders. Her long hostess gown of some shiny green material was slit to well above her crossed knees. She was, I realized, one of the aristocrats of Montmartre street life, a bar girl, ready to converse pleasantly with any man willing to pay fifty francs for eight francs' worth of cognac. Other favors came much higher.

"There must be a phone over there. I'll call the police."

"All right. We'll make a dash for it."

"No, Dottie." He turned his harassed face toward me. "They're looking for the two of us. Better if we split up until the cops get here. If I could think of someplace better than this to hide you—"

He looked at a sign, much scrawled over with phone numbers, affixed to the dirty stairway wall beyond the gate. Beneath an arrow, pointed upwards, were the words "Le Club Reno." Even though the gate was padlocked, Eric tugged at it. It did not budge.

136

"If there was only some way to . . ."

For another moment he looked down at me. Then he grasped the waistband of my skirt with both hands and began to double it over upon itself. "Eric! What on—"

"Dottie, I know what I'm doing. Even if they do see you, they won't recognize you." He stepped back a little and looked at the hem of my skirt. I, too, looked. It reached the middle of my thighs. "Lipstick," he said in that harried voice. "You're not wearing lipstick." He began to fumble in my shoulder bag. "Where's . . . Oh, here it is."

"Let me." I realized his intention now. Hand shaking, I rouged my mouth. He looked at me critically, then reached out and mussed up my short hair with both hands. "More eye stuff. You got more eye stuff with you?"

While he held my small mirror for me, I put liner on both my upper and lower lids, all the time afraid that I would stab myself in the eye. When I'd added a heavy layer of green eye shadow and stiffened my lashes with mascara, I looked at the results. A long wig would have been more effective, but perhaps the tousled hair would get me by.

I said in a shaking voice, "What if some man stops?"

"Tout him off, somehow. Nothing will happen to you. It won't take me more than a minute to phone the cops. After that I'll watch you from across the street until they get here."

He turned, stepped out onto the sidewalk. After looking quickly to his right and then his left, he crossed the street toward that intimate little bar. I saw him speak to the white-jacketed bartender, and then move out of my line of vision. In a few minutes he reappeared, again spoke to the bartender, and sat down facing the street, two stools from the girl in the green hostess gown.

I stood there, racked with indecision. My instinct was to shrink as far back as possible against that grilled barrier. But I knew that such behavior, untypical of the girls on this street, might attract a closer scrutiny from someone in a slowly cruising car. Better to move forward and stand boldly in the doorway, trusting that the gaze of the men in the dark green Ford would pass right over me.

What, I wondered dazedly, would my family think of me now? I, Dorothy Wanger, daughter of Professor William Wanger, niece of United States Senator John Wanger, standing here in a doorway, booted and mini-skirted and plastered with makeup in the guise of a Montmartre tart.

With a mixture of thankfulness and chagrin, I saw that should I take up this line of work, I probably would go hungry a lot. Male passers-by looked at me from the corners of their eyes, but kept on walking. What would happen, though, if one did stop? True, I had a tactic in mind, but would it work? And what if a couple of those girls in their own doorways along this street charged down upon me, flailing with handbags and boot heels and fingernails? I had heard they took a dim view of competition that appeared out of nowhere.

I saw that across the street the auburn-haired girl had moved onto the stool next to Eric's.

A man was coming down my side of the street. He was middle-aged, overweight, and, to judge by the cut of his rather wrinkled light blue suit, an American. He looked at me appraisingly as he passed. Then he halted and came back.

He said, "Bong jower, mah pateet." Apparently having exhausted his French, he added, in Texas-accented English, "How much, girlie?"

With a sinking sensation in the pit of my stomach, I embarked upon my contingency plan. I stretched my lips into a wide grin meant to suggest, if not idiocy, then at least severe retardation. "Gee, misder!" By forcing air up into my nose, I achieved the tone of one suffering from either a bad cold or a horrendous set of adenoids. "You mean id? I'm here from Detroid, and somebody picked my pockid. I been stadding here on my feed for aid days, and nobody bud you has—"

"My God, no wonder," the man said, and hurried on.

I leaned back against the door jamb, feeling weak. Then I looked across the street and saw that the bar girl had put her hand on Eric's knee. What was more, he was smiling at her. Perhaps he had not even seen how skillfully I had dealt with my first, and I hoped my last, John. True, he had to play the game over there, lest that burly bartender toss him into the street before the police arrived. But it seemed to me that his smile appeared a little too genuine.

And then, with an almost painful leap of my heart, I saw a dark green Ford angling out of the traffic toward the curb. No use to tell myself to stand my ground. Already I had shrunk back as far as I could into the angle between the stairway wall and the steel gate.

The slam of one car door, then another. Feminine voices, unmistakably Middle Western—Kansan, perhaps, or Nebraskan. Shakily I moved out of my corner.

The dark green Ford, license number seven-seven-six-zero, stood at the curb. Four middle-aged women, three of them plump and one of them very thin, had crossed from the car to stand giggling before that display of scarlet bras and bikini briefs and nightgowns.

Four women, out on a spree through wicked Paris in a rented Ford from Hertz, or maybe Avis.

Still shaking, I crossed the street. Evidently Eric, too, had seen the car's occupants, for he came out onto the sidewalk to meet me.

"Dottie, don't look like that. I just saw a dark green Ford coming toward us. You couldn't expect me to stand there and wait to see who was in it, could you? We both might have been shot."

His words were reasonable enough. And he had risked what he thought was death to protect me, standing there in the doorway with his defenseless back turned to the street. Nevertheless, I still felt angry. Perhaps it had something to do with that bar girl. "We'd better get back to the flat," I said.

He looked over my shoulder. "We'll have to wait minute."

I turned. A police car with two uniformed men in the front seat had drawn up near the entrance to the bar. "Better let me handle them," Eric said. "It'll just confuse matters if we both try to explain."

Eric walked to the police car and bent down to talk to its occupants. I stood there, feeling like a fool with my tousled hair and hiked-up skirt, but knowing that I would look even more of a fool if, right there on the sidewalk, I tried to restore my appearance to normal. From where I stood I could see the faces of the two policemen, stonily suspicious as they listened to Eric. Every once in while one or the other of them threw an equally distrustful look at me. Distraught as I was, I still felt a familiar sympathy for the French police. Burdened with all sorts of responsibilities, such as the issuance of business licenses, which bring them into conflict with ordinary citizens, they are aware of how much they are disliked. Consequently, they are always on the alert lest someone try to make fools of them.

I saw Eric, still talking, take out his passport and hand it to the men in the car. A moment later he extracted something from his wallet, probably his work permit, and handed it over. Finally the man in the passenger seat, still stony-faced, returned the documents to him. The car pulled away from the curb and headed toward the little square.

Eric walked back to me. "It's all right," he said. He took my arm, and we began to walk rapidly toward

141

the corner. "They knew about us."

"About the trouble in the police station?"

"Yes. Yesterday afternoon their orders to pick us up were canceled, and they were told instead to keep an eye out for dark green Fords."

Evidently the men in the patrol car were still suspicious of us, though, because before we reached the end of Rue Pigalle, they had reappeared, driving as slowly as possible on the other side of the street. At the corner they turned with us and parked across the street opposite the wrought-iron gate.

Presumably Eric's concierge was as unflappable as the rest of her kind. Nevertheless, her face was what is sometimes called a study as she took in my altered appearance and the police car parked across the street. Without comment, though, she allowed us through the gate. Almost running now, we went up the broad path between the pleasant old houses.

When we reached the front door, we heard the phone ringing. Eric twisted the key in the lock, dashed into the living room, and snatched the instrument from its cradle.

"Everything's fine here," I heard him say. "No, it's been perfectly quiet—Bettzinger? He's upstairs in the bathroom. You want me to try to get him down to the phone, or— Okay, I'll tell him. And we'll all be ready at two o'clock."

Chapter 15

WITH every seat in economy class filled, the big plane soared westward over the Atlantic. It was a perfect day for flying. Whenever I had the chance, I stole a glance through a porthole. Blue, wrinkled ocean far below, and hovering above it, casting the shadows of their bases on the water, cumulus clouds in fantastic shapes—tremendous towers, and floating islands complete with ragged shores, mountain peaks, and valleys.

But I had little time for gazing out of portholes. The hundred-odd Japanese aboard, although courteous—the older ones even made those polite hissing sounds when I gave them their dinner trays—were also demanding. They seemed to regard me, not just as a waitress, but as a kind of walking encyclopedia. How many people jumped off the Empire State Building last year? Were there bar cars on subway trains? Could one take out an insurance policy against getting mugged?

I did not mind their questions, any more than I minded moving up and down the aisle almost at a dogtrot in order to serve drinks and food to all those people. The work was a distraction from thoughts of those three nightmarish days in Paris.

True, my last two hours there had passed peacefully enough. Shortly before two, Carl Bettzinger had reached the flat, still a little pale and shaken, but fully ambulatory. At two a Columbia official had appeared, together with another Columbia security man and a plainclothes detective from the Paris police. In a Columbia car, a Mercedes, the six of us drove through light traffic to Roissy.

To the casual eye, the airport would have appeared much as it did on any day. Only those who worked there, probably, were aware that an unusual number of watchful-eyed men moved through the waiting room, walked casually up and down beside the ticket counters, or sat in the boarding lounge assigned to passengers for the three-o'clock flight to New York. Perhaps only employees, too, were aware that more than the usual number of guards were on hand to frisk male passengers, fluoroscope handbags and carry-aboard luggage, and, holding the electronic buzzer at a discreet few inches' distance, make sure that none of the women passengers had weapons concealed beneath their clothing.

At the entrance to the boarding lounge, Eric and I had parted, he to take his place among the waiting passengers, I to wait with the other men in an unused boarding lounge until the plane was ready to close its massive doors and taxi to the runway.

Now, as I moved to the front row of four-across

seats to flip over the movie screen affixed to the bulkhead, I thought of Eric up there in first class, along with expense-account biggies and two no-doubt delighted Japanese traveling on economy-class tickets. I wondered again which of the male passengers visible to me occupied seats originally assigned to the two Japanese. I had not been able to spot them for sure, although I suspected a young man in an aisle seat on the port side of the plane, now flipping through a copy of *Sports Illustrated,* and an older man on the starboard side, also in an aisle seat, who had spread out papers from his briefcase on his seat tray. Whoever my—and the plane's—guardians were, I was grateful to them, and equally grateful to the watchful-eyed men I knew had been stationed at Kennedy to make sure that nothing happened to me after I left the plane.

Somehow I had managed to banish the thought that had plagued me the day before, and the day before that—the thought that all these defenses had been marshaled against an enemy who might have no existence outside my own mind. After all, I had not lied. I had described what I believed to be true events. If the airline and the customs people and the Paris police, more aware than ordinary citizens of how bizarre twentieth-century existence had become, had thought it prudent to place some credence in my words, then the responsibility was theirs, not mine.

True, it looked now as if I might never know for certain whether those experiences in Paris had been real or fantasized. But that was my personal problem, one that I would face, along with other problems, when this trip was over and I sat alone in my apartment.

I flipped the movie screen into position. After that I supplied two last-minute requests for headsets. Then, as the subtitles of the film came on—the same Steve McQueen picture which had been shown to Paris-bound passengers the previous Sunday night—I walked back to where Rose Quinn sat beside an elderly Japanese on the plane's starboard side. I said, "I can look at your souvenirs now."

I had been both glad and sorry when I found her aboard the plane, wearing that same gypsylike outfit, supplemented now by a new scarf. She had tied it around her throat so that the words "Maurice of Paris" were visible. I had been glad because I liked her, and sorry because I had hoped that somehow she would be able to finish out her two weeks in Paris after all.

Eagerly she bent and tugged a Columbia flight bag from under the seat ahead of her. While the Japanese next to the window sat with earphones in place and eyes riveted to the screen, she spread her purchases out on her lap. The gloves for Mother and Aunt May looked serviceable enough, and the price she mentioned was less than she would have paid in a New York store. Otherwise, she had bought pure junk. More five-franc scarves, with Maurice's name on them, which I knew would go to pieces at the first washing. These, she said, were for the girls at

146

Abraham and Straus. An ash tray painted with the picture of a cancan dancer and the words "Ooh-la-la" was for her apartment house superintendent. Worst of all was the gift she had bought for her boss, the "head girl" at the wrapping desk. It was made of some gold-colored metal in the shape of Notre-Dame. The north and south towers, which could be unscrewed from the cathedral and lifted out, were to be filled with salt and pepper respectively.

I searched for a suitable comment. "I'm sure your friends are going to be delighted."

"You think so?" She hesitated a moment. "Say, do you think we could have a drink or something after the plane lands? I mean, Versailles and so on was great, but I was alone all the time, and so the best time I had in Paris was that dinner we had."

That got to me. "I'll be busy after the plane lands. But suppose we have dinner in New York soon."

"Say, that would be great. Call me anytime. The number's in the Queens book. Michael Quinn, on Berthold Street. Mother kept it under Dad's name after he died. She's afraid of obscene phone calls."

"Wise of her."

"You know, I'm going to start saving money right now, so that I can go to Paris again. Maybe I can get on your plane next time, too."

No point in telling her that I had made my last New York-to-Paris flight. "Maybe you can," I said, and moved along the aisle.

In the galley, Mimi and I checked to make sure that everything was ready for the pre-landing snack

—hot muffins and jelly, plus tea or coffee—with which Columbia seeks to hold the affections of the traveling public. Obeying the instructions of the airline and the police, I had told neither Mimi nor any of the stewardesses about the events of the past three days. And so far, although she had noticed the unusual security measures at Roissy, apparently she had not connected them with me. But her curiosity about where I had spent those three days had been increased by the sight of Eric boarding the plane that afternoon.

"Come on. What gives with you two?"

"I told you. Nothing gives. The Foundation people have called him back to New York, that's all."

"And I suppose you weren't with him these past three days. I suppose you were on a religious retreat or something."

She seemed genuinely angry, with spots of color in her cheeks. Suddenly I realized that she hadn't been joking about her feeling for Eric. She really wanted to know whether he and I were back together again. If we were not, there might be a chance for her.

She slammed a drawer shut. "I can't stand secretive people." She moved out of the galley, crossed to the single seat on the port side, and sat down.

Well, soon it surely would be all right to tell her why Eric had boarded this flight. And I would tell her, too, that as far as I was concerned, he was all hers.

I crossed to the single seat on my side of the plane, sat down, and peered beneath the half-lowered porthole blind. Outside this dimly lighted plane cabin, with its row upon row of passengers looking in rapt silence at the screen, it was still broad daylight. The water, though, had taken on the warmer glitter of late afternoon. No clouds now. And according to Jim Henderson's latest advice over the intercom, New York was clear, with a temperature of sixty-nine degrees. An easy landing ahead.

And what then? If no trouble developed at Kennedy, as seemed overwhelmingly likely now, would Columbia keep me on? Or would they, after a suitable interval, find a plausible excuse for ridding themselves of a stewardess who could be suspected of mental instability? Perhaps no airline would want me. Well, I had a college degree, and there were other jobs besides being an airborne waitress and practical nurse. Often I had discussed with Eric the possibility of my trying for a job in publishing. Maybe I would do that now.

Eric. No use to try to pretend I did not know why Mimi and other women were attracted to him, despite his absent-mindedness, his akwardness, and his occasional hot temper. In these days of sometimes brutally casual one-night stands, they appreciated his stubborn, protective attachment to me.

If it had not been for a certain morning in Bridgehampton, I would have appreciated it, too, for the rest of my life. But always in one corner of my mind I would stand in a bedroom doorway looking at my husband and my own sister asleep. And since that was the case, it was better for both our sakes that a

149

few hours from now, at my apartment, we say good-bye for the last time.

The movie was almost over. I got up and went into the galley. From then on, Mimi and I and the other girls worked furiously, carrying filled trays and empty ones and coffeepots and teapots up and down the aisle, our progress constantly impeded by passengers moving to and from the rest rooms. When the plane went into a long, gliding descent over Connecticut, we were still gathering up headsets.

The seat belt and no-smoking signs came on, reinforced by Jim's voice over the intercom. The plane shuddered as its wheels came down. Wearing my navy blue bowler now, I moved along the still-crowded aisle, herding passengers into their seats. Then I went back to my single seat and strapped myself in. Below us the beaches of Far Rockaway, pinkish with pre-sunset light, seemed to tilt as the plane banked its wings.

"Dottie!" It was a despairing cry from somewhere behind me.

I turned around in my seat. Rose's face was peering around the edge of a rest room door. Oh, Lord! What had happened? A stuck zipper on her girdle? In another few minutes the plane would be gliding steeply toward the runway. She might easily fall and injure herself.

Swiftly I unbuckled my seat belt, rose, and started toward her.

That was the last thing I remembered.

Chapter 16

Even with my eyes still closed, I was aware that my head throbbed with each pulse of my blood. When I opened them, fluorescent light gleaming on mirror glass and stainless steel made the pain worse. I closed my eyes and waited for a moment, aware by the silence and the lack of motion that the plane was on the ground. Then, steeling myself against that stab of pain, I again opened my eyes.

What was I doing, crumpled up here on the floor of one of the tiny rest rooms? Had I fainted?

I was lying on my side. Placing one palm and then the other on the floor, I raised myself to a sitting position. After a while I was able to focus my blurred vision on the dial of my watch. Six forty-seven. The plane must have been on the ground for at least half an hour, probably longer. To judge by the silence, there was no one out there in the cabin beyond the rest room door. Why was it that all those hundreds of people, including Mimi, had gotten off the plane without me?

Cautiously I raised my hand to my throbbing head. My bowler hat was gone, and I could feel a small sticky patch on the back of my head. I took my hand down.

For a moment I stared blankly at the blood on my fingers. How had I managed to injure my head? When I fainted, had I struck my head against the edge of the washbasin cabinet or the toilet seat?

It was not until then that I became aware of the long challis skirt and jacket lying crumpled on the floor beside the washbasin cabinet. No, only the lower part of each garment lay limp and crumpled. Through the bosom and around the hips the clothing seemed to have retained the plump shape of its owner. Padded? Yes, it must be.

Memory returned then. Rose Quinn, calling frantically for my aid. I had started toward her. Even though I could not remember it, I knew what must have happened after that. Once I had gone inside the little room, she had snatched the hat from my head. With the other hand—holding what weapon?—she had knocked me unconscious.

I managed to get to my knees. Hands grasping the wash cabinet's edge, I hoisted myself erect. Still clinging to the cabinet, I looked into the mirror. My white-faced reflection seemed to swim before my eyes. Feeling nauseous, I lowered my gaze. On the flat metal surface to the right of the basin lay pink butterfly glasses and a wig of coarse black hair threaded with gray. To the left lay crumpled paper towels stained with suntan makeup, several wads of cotton, and grains of some puttylike substance, also stained with makeup. Cotton to give that lumpy appearance to her jaw, putty to alter the shape of her nose, and, slathered over it all, liquid suntan powder.

A wave of dizziness struck me. I fought it off. I must not faint, because Rose Quinn—or whatever her name was—was out there somewhere, no longer a plump brunette well into her thirties, but a slender blonde in my navy blue bowler and the navy blue uniform she had worn beneath her padded skirt and jacket.

I turned the cold water tap on. Because I knew it would hurt too much to bend over, I filled my cupped hands and dashed water onto my face, not caring that I splashed my jacket in the process. I pulled a paper towel from the slit and patted my face dry. Then I opened the rest room door.

Still no sound. Only row upon row of orange upholstered seats stretching emptily away. Now that the blowers were off, the air was warm and stale. Through a porthole I could see the tall glass windows of the Columbia terminal.

Clutching a seat back every now and then for support, I moved down the aisle. Discarded magazines and newspapers and soft drink cups lay in the aisle and on some of the seats and the space between the seats. Obviously the cleaners as yet had not serviced the plane, at least not this part of it.

When I reached the seat Rose Quinn had occupied, I halted. Wedged between her seat and the one the elderly Japanese had occupied was the Notre-Dame salt-and-pepper set.

Why had she removed it from her flight bag before

leaving the plane? After a moment I realized why. She wanted to get through customs fast, and with a minimum of conversation. Any customs man, especially when inspecting the luggage of an airline employee, would have taken that gadget apart to make sure it held no drugs or other contraband.

Customs. Pray God she had not gotten through customs. I moved on into the section with blue upholstered seats. More litter, more stale air, but no people. Then, when I was about a third of the way through the last economy section, I heard the voices of men. Evidently they were coming down the covered gangway that led from the terminal to the plane's open door. A moment later I saw them in the entryway between economy and first class, two men in Columbia Airlines coveralls, one carrying a tank-type vacuum cleaner and a push broom, the other buckets which, I knew, must contain brushes, liquid soap, and window glass and upholstery cleaner. I called out to them, and quickened my pace.

That was a mistake. A wave of nausea struck me, and I knew how Carl Bettzinger must have felt when he collapsed back onto the doctor's couch. I sank onto an aisle seat and rested my forehead against the back of the seat ahead.

The two men were beside me now. One of them said, "What is it, miss?" and the other one said, "Hell, man, look at the back of her head."

I took my forehead away from the seat back. "Stop her. A girl. Tell everybody." My brain was not working very well. I tried again. "She's dressed like a stewardess, but she isn't. She slugged me. Don't let her get away."

I saw dawning comprehension in the face of the older man, the one with the vacuum cleaner. "I'll stay with her, Joe. You go find a security man, quick."

When the younger man had gone, the other one began to push up armrests in a four-across row of seats. "You'd better lie down."

I don't know how long I lay there on my side in the hot, silent plane, eyes closed, but aware of the man sitting in the seat directly across the aisle. Less than five minutes, I suppose. My time sense, like my brain, seemed scrambled. Finally I heard rapid footsteps on the gangway. I sat up. Two men in dark business suits moved toward me. They had that short-haired, clean-shaven, F.B.I. look, which was not surprising, since Columbia security men often are ex-F.B.I. agents.

They also looked frightened. I knew that only a small part of their concern was for me. I asked, "Does customs—"

"They've been notified," one of the men said curtly. "Think you can walk, or shall we send for a stretcher?"

"I can walk."

With each man supporting one of my elbows, I moved dizzily up the gangway and along a wide, almost deserted corridor. We went through the customs shed, where long lines of people still stood at the counters, and then rose in an elevator to the departures lounge. As we climbed a broad, gently

155

sloping ramp, people coming toward me seemed to move with an odd swimming motion through the pale fluorescent light. I was aware of their startled expressions, but I did not mind. All my energy was concentrated upon putting one foot before the other and fighting down nausea.

A blond young man with hornrims seemed to waver toward me. As he drew closer, I saw that he was not Eric.

Eric! Waiting all this time in the coffee shop . . .

"There's a man, Eric Lang. I was supposed to meet him in the coffee shop."

"Lang? The man you were with in Paris? We'll see that he's told."

They stopped at a door. In the small room on the other side of it they sat me down on a dark red leather couch. I saw an examining table a foot or so away. Across the room stood a sink with glass-doored cupboards above it. The emergency room. I had known Columbia maintained such a room, but until now I had not known even its location.

One of the men said, "The airport doctor's been notified. He'll be here any—"

The door opened. A short man with graying brown hair came in, glanced at me, and then said to the two men, "Out."

"Make it as fast as you can, doc. She's needed for questioning."

"Out."

They left, closing the door behind them. The doctor took a bottle down from one of the cupboards, poured part of its contents into a glass, and handed the glass to me. "Down the hatch." The cloudy liquid stung my nose and throat, but almost instantly my queasiness abated, and my mind seemed to clear a little. Hands under my armpits, he helped me to rise, and then sat me down on the examining table.

"Lie down. On your stomach." A few moments later he said, "It doesn't seem too bad."

Easy enough for you to say, I thought.

"You'll need three stitches, though. I'll have to shave off some of your hair."

I lay there, thinking bitter thoughts about Rose Quinn, while he bathed and stitched the wound and affixed a bandage.

"All finished. Know what she hit you with?"

"No."

"Well, lie down over there. You'll be almost as good as new in a little while."

I had just stretched out on the couch when the door opened and one of the security men came into the room. "All finished, doc?"

"Yes. The wound was only superficial."

If this was what a superficial wound felt like, I thought, I'd hate to have the serious kind.

"Can she come with us now?" The other man, I realized, must be waiting outside the door.

"Is it important?"

"Extremely important."

The very quietness of his voice gave me a sinking sensation. So she had gotten past customs. She was out there somewhere, that girl with almost-my-face, on God knew what errand.

"Then it's up to her." The doctor turned to me.

157

"How do you feel?"

"Good enough." I got to my feet.

My legs no longer felt rubbery, and my headache had subsided to a faint throbbing. With the two men I moved up the slanting corridor into the main waiting room. People seemed to be walking normally now, not with that swimming motion. I said, "Does Eric Lang—"

"He's waiting for us."

"Where?"

"Right here." We had halted in front of a door. Another man with a nineteen-fifties crew cut stood beside it. "Everybody's here in the V.I.P. lounge."

Chapter 17

THE sign on the door was not that crude, of course. It said "Commodore Club. Members Only." In the big, softly lighted room on the other side of the door, no white-coated bartender stood behind the small bar, and no movie stars or U.N. ambassadors or multimillionaires sat in the deep leather armchairs or at the desks lining one wall. Somebody had moved one of the desks to the center of the room. I recognized the man who sat behind it, although I knew him only by sight. He was Mr. Gaylord, head of Columbia security.

I knew some of the people who sat in the luxurious chairs, now arranged in a rough semicircle facing the desk. Mimi was there, a stricken, bewildered look in her brown eyes. Jim Henderson, minus his usual easygoing air, sat next to her. A slender, balding man I recognized as one of the customs inspectors was there. He looked not only frightened but almost sick. And Eric was there. As if too tense to sit, he stood against the wall at one end of the semicircle of chairs. I did not know who the other half-dozen or so men

159

in the room were, but I assumed that at least one or two of them were airline officials.

Mr. Gaylord said, "Do you feel up to answering a few questions, Miss Wanger?" He was a dark-haired, wide-shouldered man of perhaps forty-five. Unlike some of the strictly square types under his command, he sported modish sideburns.

I nodded.

"Then sit there, please."

He indicated a vacant chair directly opposite him. As soon as I sat down, Eric walked over to the man on my right. "Mind if I sit here?"

From the startled look the man gave him, I guessed that he must be at least a Columbia vice president or a captain of detectives on the New York police force. But he got up and moved to a vacant chair at one end of the row. Seated beside me, Eric said in a low voice, "Don't let them keep you here if you feel dizzy or anything."

"I'm okay."

Mr. Gaylord said, "Now, Miss Wanger, this woman who struck you with a flashlight—"

"Was that what it was?" Easy enough, I thought, for her to take it out of that big plastic handbag of hers and conceal it in those voluminous garments before she went back to the rest room.

"Yes. We found it in one corner of the rest room. Now, had you seen this woman before today?"

"Yes. She was on the Paris flight last Sunday night. She said her name was Rose Quinn."

He nodded. "That was the name on the plane's manifest for both flights."

"On Monday night she turned up at this little restaurant in the St. Germain district, and we had dinner together."

Why, I asked myself, had she risked having dinner with me, when some little thing—a slip of the tongue, perhaps—might have set me wondering about her? Almost instantly I realized why. It had not been the man with cactus who had drugged me. It had been Rose. While I was in the phone booth trying to call Jim Henderson, she had dropped something into my wine.

"And later that night," I went on, "I saw her again, only I didn't know it was her."

He nodded. "Yes, we know about that. Now, when you had dinner with her, did she tell you anything about herself?"

"A lot. She works—I mean, she said she works—at Abraham and Straus. She said she lived with her mother and her aunt on Berthold Street in Queens. On the plane this afternoon she said that the phone was listed under the name of Michael Quinn."

"She gave the Berthold address when she bought her round-trip ticket. A Michael Quinn lives there, all right, but he's a young bus driver with a wife and three small children. We're still checking, but evidently he has no connection with all this. Now, what sort of accent did she have?"

"I guess you could call it a Brooklyn accent. Oh, I don't mean she said 'Thoid Avenue,' or anything like that. But she said 'sawr' and 'lawr' and 'chawclate.' That sort of thing."

"And when you saw her later that night, without

her wig and makeup? What did she sound like then?"

I searched my drug-hazed memory of that night—her oddly familiar face looking down at me through the lamp's red glow. "Get up, Dorothy. We're going out." I could recall the words, but not their actual sound.

"I don't know," I said helplessly. "Since it made no impression on me, maybe it was just an ordinary American accent. You know, the kind radio and TV broadcasters are suppose to use."

He nodded and then asked, "So you gained no idea of where she might be from, or what her real nationality is?"

"No." Then I added, "Yes, one thing. In the restaurant, she used the word 'lift' instead of elevator. I'd thought that perhaps being on the other side of the Atlantic had gone to her head and she was being a little pretentious. But maybe it was a slip. Maybe she's English."

The man Eric had ousted from his chair said, "One thing's for sure. Whoever she is, she's one hell of an actress."

How true, I thought bitterly. She had made that Queens apartment she shared with her "awfully religious" mother and Aunt May completely real to me. I had been able to imagine, not only the Castro convertible where she slept, but dried strawflowers in a vase on the TV set, and religious pictures on the walls, including perhaps one of those painted Christs with eyes that give the illusion of following you around the room.

162

"Now, Jerry." Mr. Gaylord had turned his attention to the customs inspector. "Tell us what happened at your counter."

"Well, she got there early, among the first five or six in line." He looked at me. "You . . ." He paused and then said in a confused tone, "I mean, she was wearing dark glasses. She put her purse and flight bag on the counter. I said, 'No suitcase?' and she said, 'I traveled light this trip.' I didn't think anything of it. Some of the girls leave enough clothes in Paris or London or wherever so that they can travel light when they want to. What did strike me as odd was the stuff in her flight bag. Along with a nightgown and underclothes and two new pairs of gloves, there were some cheap scarves and a cheap ash tray. Stewardesses usually don't bring back that sort of tourist junk. But I figured maybe she had to buy presents for a few people, and felt too broke at the moment to buy anything good. Anyway," he said defensively, "I didn't think it was anything to hold her there for."

"Sure, Jerry." Mr. Gaylord's voice was soothing. "Nobody's blaming you. If the man at the passport desk didn't catch that phony passport made out to Dorothy Wanger, and he didn't"—he shot a glance at some man sitting several chairs to my left—"then it's no wonder you let her go by."

He paused and then turned to Mimi. "Miss Deillman, you saw her leave the customs shed, didn't you?"

"Yes. I had just joined the line at one of the counters. I saw Dorothy—I mean, the girl I thought was

163

Dorothy—moving toward the waiting room beyond the customs shed. I called out to her. She turned and said something I didn't hear, and kept on going."

She looked at me. There were tears in her eyes. "I thought you were sore at me. And all the time you were lying back there . . ."

I gave her a shaky smile. I knew she was expressing, not just sympathy, but apology for her flare of temper in the plane's galley.

A man somewhere to my right said, "Well, whatever they're up to, it must be something pretty big. They went to a lot of expense and a lot of trouble—dangerous trouble—to pull this off."

A brief silence settled down. The room seemed full of unvoiced questions. Who was she, this girl who had made herself look enough like me so that she could slip undetected off the plane and through passport and customs inspection? When the bald man had said critically, "The nose isn't quite—" Gastand had answered, "That can be fixed at the last minute." I pictured her there in the plane's rest room, with me lying crumpled on the floor. After she had removed the Rose-Quinn makeup, she must have altered the shape of her nose with a bit of expertly applied putty, and then covered her face with liquid powder similar in shade to what I always wore on duty.

But why? What was her purpose here?

Far from having collaborated with her and that strange crew in Paris, I had been their chief victim, at least up until now. No, not the chief one. An el-

derly night clerk had been that. But certainly I was
a victim. And yet, sitting here with these puzzled and
alarmed people, I had a sense of guilt, as if my stupid-
ity somewhere along the line, or my negligence, had
helped create the nameless threat that hung over us.
And not only us, but perhaps this whole city, perhaps
even . . .

What I felt must have shown in my face, because
Mr. Gaylord said, "You must not blame yourself, Miss
Wanger. It is obvious that they involved you in all
this only because you bore a strong resemblance to
that other young woman. And in Paris you certainly
did your best, often against great difficulty, to alert
the authorities."

Eric's voice was sharp. "Can't you let her go? I
don't think she looks too well."

After a moment Mr. Gaylord said, "Well, all right.
Best to stay in your apartment, Miss Wanger, tonight
and tomorrow. It's not that we're worried about you.
Obviously you have served your purpose, as far as
those people are concerned. But we'll have more
questions. And if we're lucky, we'll want you to make
identifications."

"All right. I'll stay in my apartment." What did
they expect me to do, with three stitches in my scalp?
Go water skiing?

"Your suitcase is over there beside the door," he
went on. "We wanted to save you the trouble of
collecting it yourself."

Was that their sole reason? Or had they made an
unusually thorough search of my belongings, looking

165

for evidence that I had been, after all, a collaborator rather than a victim? Well, one scarcely could blame them for that.

Hand under my elbow, Eric guided me from the room.

Chapter 18

W E reclaimed Eric's suitcase from one of the lockers near the coffee shop. Outside the terminal we found that it was fully dark now, and that sheets of newsprint and other trash, propelled by a brisk breeze, were scuttling down the road between the terminal building and the parking areas.

In the employees' parking lot I handed the VW's keys to Eric. While he unlocked the car, I glanced upward. Evidently no wind stirred the upper regions of air, because the sky was thinly veiled with smog, stained yellowish by the city's lights. Through it I could see a wan-looking half moon, and a few of the brighter stars.

Neither of us spoke until we had threaded our way through the airport's complex of entrance and exit roads, and were headed toward Manhattan. Then Eric said, "I ought to take you to a hospital."

"No. The agreement was that I was to go straight to the apartment. Besides, I'm feeling much better."

"Well, as soon as we get there, I'm going to call

your doctor. And this is one time he'll make a house call."

"I know, or you'll punch him in the nose."

"Damn right."

Strange, I thought. A few hours ago I had been sure that by now Eric would have left me at the apartment and made his final exit from my life. But here we still were, side by side. I felt a hysterical impulse toward laughter. What if there was something to that chatter of Mimi's about Sun Signs?

We were crossing the Triborough Bridge now. Like a pile of various-sized blocks constructed by some gigantic child, Manhattan glittered against the night sky. Was that girl out there somewhere among those millions of lights, still wearing a Columbia uniform? No, she would have rid herself of that by now. Had she left the airport in a taxi, or had associates picked her up in a private car? And where were they headed? The U.N. Building? Washington, D.C.? Some atomic installation?

For the first time, I felt the full impact of what might happen. It left me numb. But beneath the numbness was a whimpering protest. Like a pedestrian who feels the mugger's crooked arm around his neck, I thought, "It's not fair. Why was I the one picked?"

I said aloud, "There are hundreds of stewardesses. But just because I looked a lot like her, this had to happen to me."

Eric spoke slowly. "I've been thinking. What if we've all got the whole thing backward."

"Backward?"

"Yes. We've all figured that Gastand and the others, for God only knows what reason, looked around for a stewardess who looked enough like that girl, and finally picked you. Isn't that right?"

"Of course." I remembered standing there in the room with the smoked mirrors. "You've let finding the girl go to your head," the bald man had said. And I of course had assumed he meant me.

"Well, what if it was the other way around? What if they searched until they found a girl who had a sufficiently strong resemblance to *you?*"

I remained silent as Eric paid the toll and then piloted the VW down the curving ramp to the East River Drive. "That doesn't make sense," I said finally. "It would make sense only if I were important, or had important connections."

"I know. If you were the President's niece, for instance."

I realized what he meant. I could imagine that blond girl phoning from a booth on a lower floor of the White House. "This is Dorothy Wanger, the President's niece," she might say to some secretary-to-a-secretary-to-a-secretary. "Would it be possible for me to see my uncle for a few minutes?" And then, upstairs, when he rose smiling from his desk to greet her, there would be the gun suddenly produced from her coat pocket, or handbag . . .

But the President was not my uncle. A United States Senator had been my uncle, but he, like my much less-famous father, was dead. My sister and my half-brother and half-sister each had certain achievements to their credit, but not in government nor in anything which, as far as I could see, could make them the target of any sort of plot.

And yet there was this nagging sense that Eric had hit upon the truth. All of us had been looking at the situation backward. I was not incidental to the affair, selected only because I happened to have a certain height, weight, coloring, and cast of features. Somehow I, or something about me, was central to the whole plan.

Eyes closed in my effort to concentrate, I again went over that dreamlike episode in that lavish room somewhere in Paris. As I stood docilely beside the other girl, Gastand and the bald man had discussed the discrepancies in our appearance, and how they might be remedied. Then, while I sat in a chair with a tape recorder beside me, I had spoken certain phrases at the bald man's bidding. I had a vague feeling that for at least half an hour, like some ingenious robot, I had parroted words and phrases he gave me. But I could recall only a few—"See you later," for instance, and "Hi, there. Let me in," and "I'm dying for a cup of coffee."

Obviously he had wanted to record my voice so that the blond girl could practice its intonations. But now I saw that there might have been a reason, too, for his choice of those particular phrases. Suppose that after the girl had left the plane's rest room in a uniform made complete by my navy blue bowler, Mimi or someone else had suggested that they make

170

joint plans for the evening. The phrase "See you later," accompanied by a negative shake of the head and a friendly smile, would have helped her to slip away quickly. "I'm dying for a cup of coffee" might have served the same purpose, enabling her to detach herself from unwanted company and hurry away.

But the phrase "Hi, there. Let me in." What about that?

Or had the bald man told me to say, "It's Dorothy. Let me in."? I clenched my hands in my lap, trying to remember. No, I was sure it had been just "Let me in," as if my name would not be needed, as if the one to grant entry would recognize the speaker by voice or by appearance.

Appearance.

Sitting there beside Eric, I became rigid. Judson's intercom TV, which enabled him to see anyone standing outside the gate in the high chain-link fence. Judson, my eccentric half-brother, who defended the privacy of his laboratory and living quarters, not only with an electrified fence and an alarm system, but with vicious Dobermans.

No, it was absurd to think that the blond girl, with or without companions, might be on her way to my brother's laboratory. Despite his paranoid conviction that others might try to steal the fruits of his labors, none of his experiments had produced anything of value. He and his isolated laboratory could be neither a threat nor a temptation to anyone.

I thought of my last visit to that wooden building

at the end of the rutted, rock-strewn road through the pines. He had said he had been carrying out some sort of research in the field of allergies . . .

A thought, only half-formed as yet, seemed to make my heart stop beating for a moment.

Eric had turned off onto a potholed stretch which, paralleling the East River Drive, gives access to Ninety-seventh Street. Ahead at one side of the road, just beyond an abandoned and stripped car, stood a phone booth. "Eric, stop. I have to phone."

His startled face turned toward me. "Phone who?"

"Please! Just stop!"

I was out of the car almost before it came to a halt. Inside the phone booth I pulled the door closed. At least the light worked. That was a good omen. I fumbled in my shoulder bag, took the receiver off the hook, deposited a dime. No dial tone. Vandalized, after all.

I ran back to the VW. "Stop at the next drugstore or bar."

He said, as we drove on, "We're close to the apartment. That'll be as quick, maybe quicker."

"Yes, you're right."

"What is this? Who are you—"

"My brother. Please, Eric, just let me think. And get there as fast as you can. Double-park if you have to."

We had to. At the top of the old brownstone's steps, I unlocked the front door. We climbed mahogany-railed stairs to the second floor. Inside the apartment I switched on the light in the little foyer and reached

172

for the telephone on the wall table. Fleetingly I thought of how Eric and I used to dine at this table. By means of candlelight and a few flowers, we'd always tried to make our meals pleasant, despite the foyer's cramped space and the proximity of the kitchen.

I dialed. The phone at the other end of the line rang five times. Then Judson's assistant said, "Hello."

"Hello, Bert. It's Dorothy Wanger. I must speak to Judson right away."

"Afraid you can't. He's busy."

My hand, grasping the phone, felt damp. "I must speak to him! Tell him!"

I could imagine the nervous bobbing of Bert Haliday's Adam's apple. "Well, I'll try."

I waited for perhaps two minutes. Although his eyes held puzzled anxiety, Eric stood there quietly, not trying to question me. At last I heard my brother's irritated voice. "Dorothy, if you've made me ruin that last batch of—"

"Judson, listen. About those allergy experiments of yours—"

"That's all finished. I'm about ready to publish. Now if you'll let me get back to—"

"Judson! You said you were trying to create a new —what was the word—allergen? Anyway, you hoped to find a way to sensitize people to some—"

"Dorothy, why do you call me up to discuss matters you know nothing about? Are you drunk? You sound drunk. You'd better go easy with alcohol. Our Aunt Geraldine became alcoholic, you know. Uncle John kept it from his constituents, but everyone in Washington knew it. Now please leave me alone."

"Judson! What is the substance you hope will be a new allergen? Is it heroin?"

Dead silence for a second or two. Then he asked in a high, tense voice, "Who's been filling you up with nonsense? Was it Haliday? Haliday!" I could tell that he had turned away from the phone. "Have you been—"

"Judson!" I was screaming at him now. "Tell me! Is it heroin?"

He had turned back to the phone. "Of course not!" Like a lot of people, Judson thinks that the louder he talks, the more apt people are to believe him. "Where do you get these crazy notions? Oh, I know. You and Natalie and Gale think I'm a bit off. But if you ask me—" .

"Judson, call the Marsdale police. Tell them to get out to your laboratory right away. Tell them you're in danger. There may be people on their way to—"

"What people? Nobody's going to get in unless I let them in. And if they did somehow manage to get over the fence, the Dobermans would tear them to pieces."

"Call the police!"

"Even if I did, they probably wouldn't come. They were here last week trying to snoop around. They said they were looking for some fellow who escaped from the village jail. I told them that if they ever showed up here again without a warrant, I'd sue the village for every cent in its treasury. Now leave me alone."

He hung up. Eric watched me, comprehension in his eyes now, as I again dialed Judson's number. After the phone had rung ten times, I hung up. "I'd better call the Marsdale police myself."

Desperately I searched my memory. I came up with the number of the Marsdale movie theater, and the bank, and Della's Beauty Salon, but not that of the police. Finally I called Information.

But at least the Marsdale number answered on the second ring. "Police. Officer Simpson speaking." Bob Simpson, I knew, was the younger of the two policemen who composed Chief McGuire's staff.

"This is Dorothy Wanger. Please listen carefully. My brother Judson is in trouble. Please go out to his laboratory right away."

His voice had become cautious. "He hasn't phoned us about any trouble."

"No, and he won't. I tried to get him to. But he needs help."

"Miss Wanger, the chief isn't here, but I know he'd say the same as I do. Your brother would never let us in."

My voice rose. "Then shoot the lock off the gate! He's in trouble, I tell you."

"What sort of trouble?"

For a moment I felt baffled. How to explain, quickly and clearly? "My brother has been working on a new approach to the drug problem. Not a cure for addiction. Something that would prevent people from becoming addicted in the first place."

Dead silence at the other end of the line. I said, "I think there are people on their way to try to stop all

175

that. They may destroy his laboratory and his records, and even—even kill him and his assistant. Now do you see?"

Again that silence. Almost as clearly as if I could hear the words, I imagined him thinking, "Judson Wanger isn't the only weirdo in that family."

Then he said, "Sure, Miss Wanger. I don't know when I can locate the chief. He went fishing up to Dodson's Lake today. But as soon as I do find him, I'll tell him." He hung up.

I looked at Eric in silent frustration. Should I call the New York City police, or the state police? It might take a long time to convince them, if I ever did. And already about three hours had passed since that girl had walked out of the customs shed. Perhaps she was still somewhere in the city, conferring with associates. On the other hand, perhaps even now she and God knew how many others were driving along the East River Drive, or the even more distant roads leading north. . . .

"Gaylord," Eric said.

I let out a sigh of relief. Of course. The chief of Columbia security almost instantly could set any number of law-enforcement people in motion—state and county, even federal. And there would be no need for me to give him more than the barest information.

Again I dialed and spoke to a switchboard operator. Then a voice said, "Security. Craig speaking."

"This is Dorothy Wanger."

"Oh, yes, Miss Wanger." I had never heard his

name, but I could tell from the instant alertness in his voice that he knew all about me.

"Is Mr. Gaylord there?"

"No, he's left the terminal. Are you all right?"

"Yes. I mean, I got to my apartment all right. Can you get in touch with Mr. Gaylord?"

"It might take some time. He may be downtown in a huddle with the immigration people. Or he may be on his way to his home in Westchester. When I do locate him, what shall I tell him?"

"Tell him that—that girl is probably headed for a town named Marsdale, in Columbia County. My brother, Judson Wanger, has a laboratory about ten miles east of the village. The local police know where it is. My brother is a biochemist." I went on swiftly, explaining. Then I said, "Can you act on your own authority?"

"If I have to. But it will be better and in the long run quicker if I can get in touch with the big boss. Sit tight, Miss Wanger." He hung up.

I, too, hung up and then just stood there, leaning my weight on the phone. Sit tight. It was like telling someone to sit tight in a forest filled with man-eating beasts. And, I thought despairingly, all the things that were supposed to protect against the fanged and clawed prowlers sometimes didn't help at all. Phones were vandalized or went unanswered. Computers went haywire. Police arrived too late, or not at all. And perhaps right now, Gaylord sat unreachable behind the wheel of his car, halted with a line of other motorists behind some

177

construction site or overturned truck.

And in the meantime Judson would be moving about his laboratory, brooding angrily over my phone call, darting suspicious glances at Haliday, but nevertheless placing his faith in his closed-circuit TV and his electrified fence and his Dobermans. Judson, my brilliant, peculiar brother, who had turned dour with the disappointments and the years, but who had been patient and fatherly when he was a young man and I a demanding brat toddling at his heels.

I said, "We've got to go up there. We must get them both out of that lab and clear away from there. Slug them, if we have to, and drag them out."

"You're not going anywhere except to bed. I'll go to Marsdale."

"What would be the use? You've never even seen the place, and you know how confusing those back roads are. Even if I drew you a map, it might take you a long time to find it. And certainly the Marsdale police aren't going to guide you there. They won't go near the place unless the county sheriff or the state police okay it first.

"Besides," I went on, "he'd never let you in. Now that he's sore at Natalie, I guess the only person he'd let in besides me is my sister Gale, and probably not even her."

He looked at me, his face tired and distraught beneath the overhead light. Then he said, "All right. Let's go."

Chapter 19

As if by unspoken agreement, neither of us said much as, through heavy traffic, Eric piloted the VW back to the East River Drive and turned north toward the Willis Avenue Bridge and the interlocking highways beyond. The wind had freshened. I could see ghostly whitecaps on the black river. The wind was even stronger by the time we reached the sparser traffic on Sawmill River Parkway. Whenever the highway curved, our headlights shone on wind-tossed pine branches and the swaying trunks and fluttering, pale green leaves of young maples and alders.

It was not until we had turned onto Taconic State Parkway that Eric said, "Want to fill me in?" At this comparatively late hour, and at this distance from New York City, traffic was light.

I told him about my last visit to Judson's laboratory. "He said that he was developing some kind of injection. It would give people allergic reactions—you know, facial swelling, nausea, wheezing, and so on—to something that otherwise would have no such affects."

179

"Did it occur to you that he might mean heroin?"

"No. I thought of it as just another of Judson's crackpot ideas. Then when I remembered it last Monday in Paris, I thought maybe it was an indication that he was actually insane, and that therefore maybe I—"

"I know."

Eric drove in silence for several minutes. Then he said softly, "Wow! Imagine schoolkids in this country, and maybe eventually all over the world, getting such injections just the way they get Salk vaccine shots. And later on—"

"Yes." Later on, if they tried heroin, they would feel no euphoric rush. Instead they would find themselves violently and unpleasantly ill.

"Of course," Eric said, "such an injection might have side effects that could rule out its use. There might be legal difficulties, too, if parents refused to have their kids injected. But still..." His voice trailed off. Then he asked, "What chance do you think there is that he's developed such an injection?"

"I don't know. Other things he has pinned his hopes on haven't worked out."

But if our hunch was right, someone was afraid it would work out. Not only work out, but be used as widely as that Salk vaccine Eric had mentioned.

How had word gotten out? Through Bert Haliday, undoubtedly. And in a way that was Judson's fault, keeping his assistant so confined to those twenty acres that, during his three days each month in New York, he released his accumulated tension through alcohol.

180

Perhaps like most overly quiet men, Haliday waxed loquacious when drunk. I could imagine him in New York bars, hinting, even boasting, about his own and my brother's researches. Probably most of his hearers had reacted with boredom or disbelief. But as was inevitable, his words finally had fallen on attentive ears.

Not only attentive, but alarmed. It must be something very big, one of those men in the V.I.P. lounge had said, to cause Gastand and the others to go to so much trouble and take such risks. Hundreds of millions of tax-free dollars each year was something big. And that was what groups of vicious men and women all over the world stood to lose if the white powder in which they trafficked lost its power to enslave.

Thank God, I thought, that apparently American dealers in drugs had not heard yet of what went on in that laboratory set deep in the pines. Otherwise Judson and Haliday might long since have been found dead in the smoldering ruins of their laboratory.

But how was it that Emile Lavery, if that was the bald man's name, had not seen to it that word of the formula reached drug dealers on this side of the Atlantic? True, he had deadly enemies here. But why should he care who it was who stopped the threat to the narcotics traffic, as long as it was stopped?

When Eric spoke, I realized that his thoughts had been following the same course. "Even if we're right about Judson, we're missing something—something important. Why should that guy in Paris have gone to so much trouble to keep the whole job under his control? Why did he have to bother with it at all, when he could have just seen to it that word was leaked to big-shot drug dealers in New York?"

"I don't know," I said. And anyway, divining Lavery's motives was not of primary importance now. The important thing was to reach those two men who, oblivious of their peril, were moving about the laboratory or watching TV in the shabby living room.

"And here's another thing," Eric went on. "Why did that dame slug you? Why didn't she just go through customs as Rose Quinn and later on shed the wig and the makeup and the rest of it?"

"At least I can guess the answer to that." My tone was bitter. "When I had dinner with her Monday night, I was idiot enough to tell her that I was afraid my brother was—disturbed. She said, in that friendly nosy way of hers, 'You mean you think he's nuts?' And then I explained that it was something he'd said about his experiments that worried me. I also told her I was going to call him up just as soon as I got back to New York, and demand that he explain the whole thing to me."

I remembered how she had said, "You do that, honey." And all the time she must have been thinking about the best way to keep me from doing it.

"I get it," Eric said. "They couldn't risk anything like that. They were afraid he might be talking over the phone to you in New York only minutes before their blond ringer showed up at his gate."

"Yes," I said in that same bitter voice, "and so she tried to make sure I'd be in no condition for phone

chats with anyone tonight." A
"Take the next exit."

We turned off the ramp onto
distance I could see, silhouetted a
by the light of the half moon, a lov
was orchard country. Apple tree
laden branches moving like a restless
wind-stirred dark, lined both sides of
and then I caught a whiff of their fragr
the widely spaced farmhouses we pa
lights, but most of them were dark.

Surely by now Gaylord or his assistant
the police. I kept hoping for the sound of si
the sight of a car with a revolving red roof
there was only the steady hum of the little
from-new engine, moving at its top speed of
more than seventy miles an hour past the or
and open fields and sleeping farmhouses. The
we got to Judson's place, the more tense I be
whenever I saw the dazzle of overtaking headli
in the rear-view mirror. I could tell, by the way I
kept glancing up at the mirror, that he, too, imagin
a blast of gunfire from another car's dark interio
and the VW careening off the road. But each time the
car sped past and withdrew into the distance, tail-
lights dwindling.

Had Eric's reasoning and mine been all wrong?
Was it for some quite different purpose that I had
been left crumpled and unconscious on the rest room
floor? Or had she and her confederates—terrible
thought—already managed to invade that carefully

arded twenty acres? I had a vision of the laborato-
's flames mounting into the night sky, and the Do-
ermans huddling terrified in the far corner of their
kennel.

We turned onto a narrow, paved road for about
five miles and then, after seeing no other cars whatever, turned onto an even narrower unpaved one.
No orchards or farmhouses now. Just pines and
deciduous trees crowding close to the rutted road. I
sat rigid, ears straining for the sound of another car,
eyes directed ahead and a little to the left. But I
heard no engine but our own, and saw no glow of
flames staining the night sky.

As we turned a curve, our headlights gleamed on
a corner of a tall, chain-link fence. Ahead was a wide,
glowing circle, cast by a tall floodlight set several
yards inside the gate. "Don't let him see you on the
TV," I said, "or he won't open the gate." Feeling
foolish, I realized I had spoken almost in a whisper,
as if afraid that my voice might carry to Judson, more
than a quarter of a mile back there in the pines.

Eric stopped the car several yards short of the gate.
Now I could hear the yelping of the Dobermans. The
wind, I realized, must have carried our scent to
them. Since all the barks seemed to come from one
area, I knew that they had not been released yet for
their nightly patrol of the grounds.

Eric switched off the lights. I started to get out of
the car, but he put an arresting hand on my arm. We
sat there in silence relieved only by the sough of
wind through the pines, and the distant yelping of

the dogs. No car between us and the gate light, or beyond it, on either side of the road.

We got out. Leaving Eric beside the car, I moved to the circle of floodlighted gravel in front of the gate and looked up. The eye of a camera affixed to the gate's left-hand upright stared down at me. I said loudly, to make sure my voice carried to the camera unit's concealed microphone, "Judson! Let me in."

I waited. No sound except the wind and the dogs' yelping. Why didn't he answer? Perhaps he was in the living room watching one of those noisy westerns which, for some reason, were the only sort of TV entertainment which appealed to him. In that case, he might not hear my voice emanating from the closed-circuit TV screen which hung above the door-way between the laboratory and living room.

Or perhaps, I thought, with my stomach gathering itself into a cold knot, that blond girl, with or without companions, had already been here—and gone. "Judson!" I shouted.

I heard my brother's voice, loud with irritation, over the intercom. "Dorothy, what the hell kind of game are you playing?"

"Judson! Please!"

He did not answer. After several seconds, though, I heard a buzzing sound. Swiftly I pushed one side of the gate open. Eric was already moving forward, crouched low, keeping close to the fence to avoid the camera's eye. We went through the gate. As Eric closed it, I heard the click of its locking mechanism.

Chapter 20

$\mathbf{W}$E started down the rutted, rock-strewn driveway. Although the moon was low in the west now, tilted above the black, ragged tips of the pines, it gave enough light that we could move at a swift walk without fear of stumbling. The barking of the dogs grew more frenzied. I imagined them hurling themselves at the chain-link walls of their prison and then falling back.

It was strange about the dogs. True, if they were very busy, sometimes neither my brother nor Bert Haliday remembered to release the dogs at nightfall. But one would have thought that tonight, after my phone call, they would not have kept the dogs penned. Belatedly and uneasily, I realized that Eric and I might have been a bit too hasty about going through that gate.

Soft footfalls behind us.

My heart gave a painful leap. I whirled around, aware that Eric also had turned.

There were two of them, with hat brims shadowing their faces. One was short and burly-shouldered,

186

the other thin and a few inches taller. Each man held a gun. I could see the dull gleam of the barrels. As I stared at the gun in the hand of the shorter man, the one facing me, I had a terrible awareness of how swiftly a bullet could spit from it to tear through my flesh.

The short man asked, in French-accented English, "Why are you here?"

As I looked back at him, unable to speak, I felt Eric's arm press gently against mine. It took me a second or so to realize the nature of his warning. We must pretend ignorance. If they knew why we had come here, they would know also that we must have called the police. They would finish their task here as swiftly as possible and leave. And their task would consist of killing not just my brother and Bert Haliday, but Eric and me as well.

"We came to see my brother!" I tried to put bewildered indignation into my voice, but it seemed to me that it held only terror. "What are you doing here? How did you get in?"

"Do not ask questions. Turn around."

We obeyed. I took one look at Eric walking beside me, his face white and set, his hornrims glittering faintly in the moonlight. Then I looked straight ahead and tried to gather my panic-stricken thoughts. How long had they been here? Not long, or Judson would not still be alive. And that girl. Was she here somewhere inside the fence? Probably not. As soon as she had obtained entry for her companions, probably she had slipped out through the gate to wait

187

in their car, hidden somewhere among the trees which stretched on both sides of Judson's property and across the road.

No wonder Judson had asked angrily over the intercom, "What the hell kind of game are you playing?" Only minutes earlier, he had admitted someone he believed to be me. He must have thought I had returned to my car for some reason, and then again demanded admission. But that explanation of his anger had not occurred to me until now. I had thought he was still irritated by my phone call.

That phone call. I felt cold perspiration trickle down my sides under my blouse. If they took us inside the laboratory, would Judson blurt out that I had tried to get him to call the police? He might, and thereby decrease whatever chances any of us might have of staying alive.

Behind me, the taller of the two men said in French, "Damn Lavery. If we hadn't had to report to him, we'd have been finished with this two hours ago."

"There's no use in complaining. You know how the boss is. He has to run everything, every step of the way. Besides, we were lucky. Sometimes it takes six hours to get a trans-Atlantic phone call through."

Lavery. So the bald man with the tic was Emile Lavery. Little good, I thought bleakly, that knowledge could do us or anyone now.

From the corner of my eye, I saw a gleam of white off among the trees. That playhouse where, so many years ago, Natalie and I had served pretend tea and real cookies to the young Judson. A few yards farther on, close to the road, stood the Dobermans' kennel. At sight as well as scent of strangers, they had become frenzied. I saw their dark forms leaping at the fence, falling back.

I was sure now that the dogs had been prowling the woods when that girl who looked like me had asked for admission. Before releasing the gate's lock, Judson or Bert had summoned the dogs back to their kennel. And so now, those Dobermans upon whom my poor brother had relied for protection, could do nothing but rage inside their prison. Their uproar could not even alert the two men in the laboratory. Intent upon their work, or absorbed by some cowboy-and-Indian chase on the TV screen, they must be assuming that the dogs barked at me as I moved alone down the long drive.

Through the cacophony of barks and snarls, I heard the taller man say, "Filthy brutes. I'd like to walk over there and shoot every one of them through the head."

The other man laughed. "Maybe you can, later. As the Americans say, one tends to business first, and then takes one's pleasure."

The laboratory was only a few yards ahead now. Even though Judson's living quarters were at the rear of the building, I could hear, very faintly, a TV sound track. Apparently he had left a light burning on the battered desk in his office. Its glow fell through the window onto the figure of a man who stood, dark head bare, beside the little front porch.

189

He waited, motionless, as we approached.

Even though I had not been able to give more than a vague description of him to Eric or anyone else, I recognized him instantly. The last time I had seen him he had been seated, wearing a suede jacket, in the back seat of a Ford. Now he was dapper in dark trousers and turtleneck, and a dark sports jacket. In one hand he carried a small canvas satchel.

"Well," he said, "what have we here?" His English, although accented, had an easy fluency.

The short, burly man said in French, "We picked them up just inside the gate, Jules. She says they came to see her brother."

"The boss tells me they both speak French," the man in the turtleneck said. "Not that it matters now."

Not that it matters. I had not realized that such an ordinary phrase could be so chilling.

He was more intelligent than the other two. His eyes, narrowed in speculation, moved from my face to Eric's and then back again. Eric, too, must have read the gathering suspicion in his gaze, because he said in an angry voice, "What is all this? And tell these two goons to take those guns away from our backs. They might go off."

The man named Jules looked at us for a moment more, and then shrugged. "Not if you do as you're told." He added in rapid French, "I looked through the living-room window. They're both back there."

I heard the short, burly man say, "Do you want one of us to go back to the gate?"

"No. Now that we've got two more on our hands, I'll need you both inside. I don't expect any trouble out on the road, but if there is any, Irene will give us three blasts on the horn."

Irene. So that was her name.

He added, turning toward the porch, "We'll go in this way."

The gun's muzzle nudged my back. On legs that felt numb, I followed Jules up onto the porch and through the unlatched screen door. The others, I knew, must be filing in after me, although the sound of their footsteps was covered by the now thunderous TV sound track. I heard, through the music, John Wayne's shouting voice, and the bawling of cattle. Jules seized the phone on Judson's desk, and with one swift jerk tore the wires from the wall.

We followed him into the laboratory. Light from the office behind us and the half-opened living-room door ahead shone on the empty animal cages against one wall and the long wooden table, laden with microscopes and Bunsen burners and racked test tubes, which stretched down the center of the room.

Jules pushed the living-room door wide open. At his gesture, I stepped past him into a room furnished in what Natalie once described as junk-shop eclectic. Again the chilling nudge of that gun. Aware that the others were crowding in after me, I stepped farther into the room.

Bert Haliday, fiddling with the color-control knob on the big TV set, straightened up and stared at us in slack-jawed astonishment. Judson, seated in a chair

191

with cigarette-burned maple arms, swiveled his thin face toward us. On the screen, a river of cattle flowed down a valley, watched by two mounted men on a hillside.

"Dorothy!" Judson's voice, high and thin with shock, rose above the TV's sound. "What is this?"

"I don't know." Don't mention my phone call, I was pleading silently. Don't mention my phone call. "We came inside the gate and here were these men with guns—"

"Isn't that Eric?" Shock and fear had set him to babbling. "Is he in on this? I thought you'd divorced—"

"Shut up, professor," Jules said, not unpleasantly. "Be quiet, and you won't get hurt. Haliday, shut that thing off."

At the sound of his name, the astonishment in Bert's face deepened. Adam's apple working, he stared at the man in the turtleneck.

"Shut it off, I tell you!"

Bert obeyed. John Wayne's and Montgomery Clift's faces vanished from the screen, and were replaced by a rapidly dwindling disc of light.

For a moment there was silence. Then Judson, lunging from his chair, started toward the telephone on a rickety table against one wall. Jules stepped forward and brought the side of his hand down on my brother's outstretched wrist in a karate chop. "Now go back and sit down."

Rage as well as fear in his face now, left hand grasping his injured wrist, Judson returned to his chair.

Jules set the satchel on the rickety table. Then, lifting the phone, he jerked its wires loose. "And you two," he said, his gaze going from Eric to me. "Just stand there. Don't move. Charles and Marcel have nervous fingers on a trigger.

"All right," he said, turning toward Bert, "open the safe."

Bert's face was greenish now. "Safe? What safe?"

The man in the turtleneck smiled. "You don't remember me at all, do you? I thought you might not. You were—" He paused, as if for a moment the idiom had eluded him. "You were bombed out of your skull."

The first sick comprehension had come into Bert's eyes. Jules went on, "I'm sure you remember Dave and Harry's Bar on Second Avenue, though. That's where we ran into each other one night about three weeks ago. The more drinks I bought, the more you talked. Not just about the formula, but the fence, the closed-circuit TV, the dogs, the kid sister who was the only one the professor here would let in—everything."

Bert turned his miserable gaze to Judson. "I didn't know what I was doing, Dr. Wanger. And I don't remember a thing about it."

"You told me that the safe was behind the china closet." Jules's gaze wandered around the room, stopped at a glass-fronted cabinet filled, not with china, but stacks of old magazines. "Move it out and open the safe."

"No, Bert!" My brother's voice was agonized.

193

"Keep quiet, professor," Jules said. Then, to Haliday: "Get on with it."

Shoulders sagging in despair, Bert crossed to the china closet. Its casterless claw feet shuddered over the floor as he moved it aside, revealing a small wall safe set at less than waist height. He crouched, turned the dial to the right and then to the left. Apparently he made a mistake, because he turned the dial back to locked position, wiped his palms on his trouser legs, and started over again. The room was so quiet that I could hear each tumbler as it fell.

He opened the safe, reached inside, stood up. His face a sick mask, he held out a sheaf of paper about a fourth of an inch thick, bound in lightweight blue cardboard. Jules took it.

It looked so harmless. It might have been a college theme, or the sort of handbook manufacturers provide to buyers of home freezers or lawn mowers. And yet it had already brought death to an old man one early morning on a Paris street. And now it had brought death into this shabby room. Death for Bert, standing there ashen-faced, and for my brother, hands gripping the arms of his chair, and for me, and for Eric—Eric, who, if he had not been so determined to protect me, would be safe in his Paris flat now.

Underneath my fear, I felt a surge of anguished tenderness for the man who had been my husband. I ached with longing to reach out to him, and through our clasped hands try to convey everything —love, sorrow, regret for every wasted moment. But

194

I dared not move, dared not even turn my face toward him, lest those guns held at our backs go off.

My brother, though, tormented gaze fixed on that sheaf of pages in Jules's hands, apparently did not realize his peril. Or perhaps, strange man that he had always been, he valued the results of his labors more than his own life. He said in that agonized voice, "You're not going to destroy that, are you? It represents five years' work. And I have an appointment with a man from the Narcotics Bureau down in Washington next Friday morning. I was going to show it to him."

Frowning with incomprehension as he leafed through the pages, Jules did not look up. "So your boy Haliday told me. Why the hell else would we have been in such a rush on this job? Three weeks to set up the whole thing."

Judson repeated, "You're not going to destroy it, are you?"

Jules closed the cardboard covers then and laughed. "Destroy it? We wouldn't dream of it. This is going to make my boss king of the world."

Those incomprehensible words seemed to hang in the air for a moment. Then suddenly I understood them.

On the way up here, Eric and I had puzzled over why Lavery had not arranged it so that drug dealers on this side of the Atlantic would save him the trouble of destroying my brother's work. Why hadn't we guessed that Lavery would not want it destroyed?

Oh, not that it would make him, in Jules's phrase, king of the world. Just king of the drug traffic. With that formula in his possession, Emile Lavery no longer would be just a second-rate criminal. Instead he could dictate terms to men of his kind in every country, including his feared and hated enemies in New York. Cut me in on every deal, he could say, and this formula will stay in a Swiss bank vault, and everything will go on just as before. Try to kill me, or even hold out on me, and I'll ruin the game for all of us, forever.

I watched Jules stuff the sheaf of paper down the waistband of his trousers and then button his jacket. He said in French, "Marcel, we passed what looked to me like a storeroom back there in the laboratory. See if it can be locked from the outside."

I sensed that it was the man behind me who turned and left the room. Then the significance of Jules's words brought me a half-incredulous but joyful relief. A storeroom. He was going to leave us locked in a storeroom—alive. Otherwise, why bother to lock it?

I did not know what his motives were. Surely the formula could not be valuable to Lavery for very long if its creators were left alive to repeat their work. And surely Eric and I knew far too much to be allowed to talk. But no matter why he chose to grant us our lives, as long as he did.

I did steal a look at Eric then, expecting to see relief in his face. He was staring straight ahead, face white, jaw set.

196

Footsteps behind me. "There is a lock. The key is in it."

I had not seen Jules take a gun from a pocket or from under his jacket, but there was a gun in his hand now. "All right, all of you, into the laboratory."

Chapter 21

THE man named Marcel had turned on the green-shaded, two-hundred-watt bulb which dangled from the laboratory ceiling. It still swung, its circle of light moving back and forth over the long table, the animal cages, and an open door on the other side of the room.

I went into the storeroom first. Here, too, an over-head light had been turned on. I gained a swift impression of a room perhaps fifteen feet long and six wide, with cardboard boxes piled in one corner and with wall shelves holding bottles of various shapes and sizes. High on the rear wall was a tiny window less than a foot square.

"No, not you, Haliday," I heard Jules say. "For being such a nice, cooperative fellow, we're letting you come with us."

Fleetingly, I wondered about that. Why should they take him with them? Then Eric and my brother were in the room. The door closed. A key turned in the lock. Footsteps withdrew.

Judson had sat down on the floor and rested his graying, ginger-colored head on his updrawn knees.

With his arms wrapped around his legs, he bore a heart-twisting resemblance to some catatonic patient in a mental hospital. "Judson, don't! You can do your work over."

"You don't understand." The dogs were raging again. I had to bend down to hear Judson's muffled words. "Five years. My mind's not as keen as it once was. And I need Bert. Working alone, it might take me—"

"Bert will be all right." For a chill moment I wondered if that was true. "And you can do it alone, if you have to." Straightening up, I turned. "Eric, tell him—"

Ear pressed to the door, he cut off my words with a gesture. Why did he look so white, so tense? The relief I had felt only minutes before was replaced by a nameless dread.

He said, "I think they've gone now. The dogs are quiet."

While I watched, uncomprehending, he moved swiftly to the rear of the storeroom, turned, and ran at the door, turning at the last moment to strike it jarringly with his shoulder.

"Eric! What are you—"

"Don't interfere, honey."

Again he moved to the back wall, and ran at the door. This time I saw him wince with pain as his shoulder struck the solid wood.

I caught his arm. "Eric! The police are sure to be here soon. And there's plenty of air. Anyway, we can break the glass in that window—"

"Dorothy, listen." The room was not warm, and

yet sweat glistened on his forehead. "He brought that satchel into the lab with him. Right now it's probably not more than a few feet from this door." He threw a glance at Judson's frail, huddled form.

The satchel, I thought confusedly. What did the satchel have to do with it?

And then, with my body turning ice-cold, I understood. Eric must have seen that I did, because he said, "They'll want to be at least a few miles away when it happens. I figure we've probably got about ten minutes."

I stepped away from him. Throat rigid now, I watched him run repeatedly at a door which shuddered at each bruising impact but did not give way. Judson, no longer with head sunk on his knees, watched him too, a look of half-comprehension on his face.

No need to speculate any longer about why they had not shot us. The bodies of three people, found in the laboratory's ruins, might not awaken immediate suspicion. Almost any laboratory held explosive materials. Three bullet-ridden bodies, though, would bring an immediate alert of police for miles around, and at every airport and ship dock. By leaving us alive until the bomb went off, they expected to gain enough time to get out of the country.

And no need to wonder now why they had taken Bert with them. A pair of able-bodied young men running against that door might have broken it down before Jules and the others were more than a mile or so away.

200

Bert would not be with them long. I was sure of that now. Perhaps already they had stopped, marched that poor loner a hundred yards or so into the woods, and left his body concealed in a clump of underbrush.

Eric no longer winced when his shoulder struck the door. Perhaps it had become numb. How many minutes had passed since the key had turned in the lock? Eight? Ten? More than that? One image filled my whole conscious now—that canvas satchel, with its timer ticking away our lives, in one of the empty animal cages, or on the long table, or only a few feet away on the laboratory floor.

The door gave a cracking sound as Eric's shoulder struck it. From the corner of my eye I saw Judson getting to his feet. Eric ran at the door again, and then again. With the sound of rending wood and the metallic shriek of the breaking lock, the door swung outward.

Dimly I was aware that Judson was the first to run from the storeroom. I found myself out in the laboratory, too, with Eric's hand grasping my arm. They had turned off the green-shaded globe, but enough light came from the storeroom to show that no satchel stood nearby on the floor or on the long table. Eric hesitated for perhaps two seconds. I felt I could read his racing thoughts. Should he risk a few more seconds to try to find the satchel and hurl it as far as possible from this building? No, there were too many possible hiding places. He hurried me toward the lighted rectangle of the office doorway.

Sounds from up there. Slam of a wooden drawer, squeak of a metallic one. We found Judson on his knees beside the filing cabinet, pawing through files in the bottom drawer. I cried, "Judson, get up from there!"

He turned a feverish-looking face up to us. "I've got some old notes somewhere here. They'll help me—"

"Come on!" Roughly Eric pulled Judson to his feet. "For God's sake, Dottie, move!"

I ran out to the little porch and down the steps, aware that Eric was drawing Judson after me. I heard the screen door slam. Instantly the Dobermans began to bark and snarl.

The moon was down now. A few yards beyond the square of light from the office window, the night seemed to me pitch-dark. As I passed the kennel, I could hear the Dobermans leaping at the fence, but I could not see them. I went on at a half-run, expecting that at any moment a rock would trip me up.

It was not a rock my left foot encountered, but a rut. My ankle turned, sharply and painfully, and I went down.

Almost at once Eric was beside me, lifting me to my feet. "Shall I carry you?"

"No, just help me."

With his arm supporting me, I moved forward at a hobbling run. My eyes, more accustomed to the darkness now, caught the gleam of the playhouse off among the wind-stirred trees. We moved forward another few yards.

And then the whole world seemed to light up with an orange glow. I heard an ear-shattering boom, followed by a sustained roar. I felt a rush of air as the shock wave passed us.

We turned. The building's front wall was still intact, but flames, whipped into spirals by the wind, roared upward through the broken roof. No sound from the dogs now. I knew that they must be huddled in the far corner of their kennel, whimpering with that most fundamental of animal terrors—the fear of fire.

Realization must have come to Eric a second before it did to me, because I heard him say softly, "My God." And then I, too, saw that on the rutted drive, flooded by that dancing orange light, no thin figure hurried toward us.

My ankle, I thought. It must have been when Eric hurried forward to help me to my feet that Judson had seized the opportunity. He had gone back, my foolish, stubborn brother, to get his precious notes.

"Wait here," Eric said. "Don't go any nearer." And then, tall figure silhouetted against the flames, he was running down the drive.

I screamed his name and hobbled after him, praying that I would not go down with a twisted ankle again, or trip over the jagged rocks that seemed to move in that wavering light. Another sound was knifing through the flames' roar. Sirens, far too many of them to signal the approach of Marsdale's two-car police force or one-engine volunteer fire department. State police, then. But the thought registered only dimly in my consciousness. All my attention was centered on that running figure. With terrible clarity I was realizing that, rather than have Eric risk his life, I would prefer that my brother be left to die.

My toe caught against something. I fell flat. Stunned, I lay there for a moment. Then I scrambled to my feet. My brother's slight figure had appeared in the office doorway, black against the fire raging inside the building. I saw Eric run up onto the porch. Then he was half-leading, half-carrying the older man down the steps. With horror I saw that Judson's body seemed outlined with ragged little flames. Eric drew him a few feet farther, and then threw him to the ground and dropped to his knees beside him. As I hobbled forward, I saw the rise and fall of Eric's hands, beating out those little flames.

I still had not reached the two men when those sirens dwindled to silence outside the gate.

Chapter 22

ERIC and I, leaning back in the luxury of wide seats, exchanged smug smiles. "Nothing like traveling first class," he said.

Ordinarily Columbia provided off-duty employees and their spouses with economy seats at a reduced rate. But in our case the airline, in recognition of services above and beyond, et cetera, had granted us free first-class tickets.

"Nothing like it, spouse," I agreed.

Our stewardess, a small brunette who must have been new to the airline, since I did not recognize her, took Eric's order for a Manhattan and mine for a Tom Collins. Then she said, "Congratulations."

"Thanks," Eric said, "but why?"

"Your wife's corsage." Until then I had forgotten that I still wore gardenias, pinned by Eric to the shoulder of my beige linen coat before we were married at City Hall that morning. "But even without the flowers I'd have been able to tell, just by looking at you two, that you're newlyweds."

"Well, not exactly," I thought of saying, but decided against it.

When she had brought our drinks, we raised our glasses to each other. Eric used his left hand. His right, badly burned that night three weeks before, was still bandaged. Even so, he had fared better than Judson, whose extensive burns still confined him to a hospital bed. And he had fared far, far better than poor Bert Haliday. The day after the laboratory was bombed, the police had found his body, shot through the head, about a quarter of a mile away in the woods.

The men who had blown up the laboratory that night must have thought, even after they heard the sirens screaming miles behind them, that they had excellent chances of escape. What they did not know was that the state police had set up roadblocks at each end of the long stretch of unpaved road which ran past Judson's property.

Even so, the police had been unable to save Judson's formula. At sight of the roadblock, the man who carried that sheaf of paper had doused it with cigarette lighter fluid, set it afire, and tossed it into the windy dark. The next day the police had recovered only a few fragments, charred beyond readability.

When Judson was told of his assistant's death and the destruction of their joint work, the double blow had plunged him into deep depression. But when I had visited him in the hospital two days ago, his spirits had been excellent. That was small wonder. A Treasury Department official had assured him that morning that once he was well he again could embark upon his research, this time with government financing sufficient for all the assistants he might need, and under government protection.

A man carrying a weekly news magazine came down the plane's aisle. The magazine's cover bore the photograph of some Arabian potentate. But the week before it had been my brother's thin face which had looked out from newsstands all over the country. As befitted a cover story, the magazine had reported the whole episode in depth. There had been an account of how, after the men arrested that night had been questioned, the Paris police had arrested Emile Lavery in his lavish apartment in the Auteuil district. Hours later an Interpol agent had picked up Jean-Paul Gastand in Madrid.

The most colorful of the people involved, the girl who had dined with me as Rose Quinn and later appeared in my room as a nameless blonde, rated several paragraphs. She was twenty-seven, older than she had appeared to my drugged senses that night in Paris. But I had been right about her nationality. Only offspring of a middle-class London couple, Irene Cummings had been an excellent mimic even as a child. At eighteen she had obtained a part in a long-running revue in London's West End. Later with the rest of the company she had come to the United States and, after more than a year's run in New York, had toured all the cities between there and the West Coast.

It was in San Francisco that the play's director had discovered that she had become addicted to heroin. Fired, she returned to London and joined a theatrical troupe touring European capitals. In Rome she had been fired again.

After that, apparently, she had drifted all over Europe and the Middle East. In Algiers she had met, and had a brief affair with, Jean-Paul Gastand, a handsome Frenchman whose antique business served as a cover for a far more lucrative role, that of second-in-command to the head of a small but prospering drug ring.

The stewardess, handing us the big, fancily embossed menus Columbia uses in first class, broke in on my thoughts. "I can recommend the Chicken Kiev," she said. "It would go well with the champagne. You're having champagne, of course?"

"Why, what else do people drink with dinner?" Eric asked.

She moved away down the aisle. My thoughts returned to Irene Cummings.

According to the news magazine, Gastand had forgotten all about the girl until, two years later, he had been summoned by his boss. Some man in America, some reclusive nut of a biochemist, might wreck their whole business, now and forever. On the other hand, if they met the challenge swiftly and correctly, they might achieve such profits and such power as they had never dreamed of. What was needed was a girl, a bright girl, who bore at least a fairly strong resemblance to the chemist's half-sister.

They'd had a picture of me, my graduation picture from my college yearbook. Gastand instantly had been reminded of that girl in Algiers. Even now, sitting here with Eric in this warm plane cabin high above the dark Atlantic, I felt repugnance and indignation at the thought of those two men, weeks before I knew they existed, handing my graduation picture back and forth between them.

It had taken Gastand less than a week to locate Irene Cummings, not in Algiers, but right there in Paris in a Left Bank cellar club, where each night she gave imitations of celebrities ranging from Dietrich to Streisand to Liza Minelli. To his delight he found that what change there had been in her was for the better. She was one of those rare addicts who had managed to kick the habit once and for all.

On a forged passport made out to Rose Quinn, of Queens, New York, she had crossed the Atlantic and then returned to Paris on my flight. With a familiar stir of anger I recalled how she had watched me through those butterfly glasses as I moved up and down the aisle. I had thought of her as lonely, eager to make friends. And all the time she, like any skilled mimic, had been studying my gait, my gestures, my smile.

Emily Lavery must have been right, I reflected. Gastand's pride in his protégé surely had addled his brains. Otherwise he would not have tried to alter the plan—and perhaps take over the whole enterprise—that morning there on the Paris sidewalk. Thank God, I thought with an inward shudder, that Eric and Wolfgang had been trailing me. Otherwise I would have been dead within a few hours, and it would have been Irene Cummings who recrossed

209

the Atlantic as Stewardess Dorothy Wanger, or at least tried to.

A few seats ahead and across the aisle, the brunette stewardess was pouring what looked like sparkling burgundy into a male passenger's wineglass. I was reminded of how my unwelcome dinner companion, that night in Paris, had slipped a drug into my glass of *vin ordinaire*. How would she have managed, I wondered, if I had not gone back to the phone booth to call Jim Henderson? That handbag of hers, I decided—that big brown plastic bag she had placed on one corner of the table, probably with its clasp unfastened. It would have been no trick at all for her to push it, spewing its contents to the floor. And while we both scrambled about beneath the table for her belongings, she could have surfaced long enough to drop something into my glass. Yes, probably that had been her original plan.

Eric said, "I'll bet Wolfgang will be glad to see us." During the past weeks he had been in touch with that pet shop owner both by phone and by letter.

"There's one thing wrong with that flat," he went on. "Not enough room in back for a dog that big to exercise. I hope we can find someplace not too far away where he can have a good run each morning and evening."

He meant the flat in that quiet enclave only two minutes' walk from Rue Pigalle. Feeling amused now, I thought of my anger that day when, after the four giggling women had gotten out of the dark green Ford, I had charged across the street toward the bar where he sat with the luscious bar girl's hand on his knee.

Incidentally, although Eric had been wrong that day about the dark green Ford, he had been right about the speedboat. According to Lavery's statement, two of his men—in an old black Citroen rather than a Ford—had kept track of me that last day in Paris. Their purpose, of course, had not been to try to stop me from boarding that plane, but to make sure that I did not force them to alter their plan by failing to board it. They had not followed us on the Seine, though. The men in the speedboat had been, apparently, just what Eric had judged them to be— a pair of reckless pranksters.

I looked at the man I twice had married. Maybe, I reflected, Mimi was right. I said aloud, "Maybe it's our Sun Signs."

"Our what?"

"Sun Signs. Mimi says it's because of them that we seem to be stuck with each other."

"Who cares why, as long as we are?"

I leaned close to the porthole and, shading my eyes with my hand against the cabin's lights, looked out past the pulsing red glow on the port wing to the stars glittering above the horizon. Below us, dimly visible, was an unbroken sea of clouds. Probably we would land in that familiar old Paris drizzle.

But, as Eric had said, who cared?